To

The
LEGEND
of
DEPUTY JIM

dan e. hendrickson

The Legend of Deputy Jim (this novel) is a work of pure fiction. Names, characters, places, products, businesses, organizations, incidents, situations and events (items) are either the product of the author's imagination or are used in a totally fictitious and imaginative way not based on any true or real incidents or facts, and are not intended to be an endorsement, criticism, or true report of said items. Any resemblance to actual persons, living or dead, business establishments, organizations, events, locales, and situations is entirely coincidental as all such resemblances are the fictitious products of the author's imagination. Though known facts regarding certain items may be true, such items and the scenarios in which they are found in this work and the way in which they are used is totally fictional.

ISBN: 978-0-578-56832-4

Dedication

There are so many fine upstanding law enforcement people out there and they all deserve praise. One is my dear friend Joe Arzy who served in the Wyoming Highway Patrol for most of his adult life. Joe, your knowledge of our mutual hometown of Sheridan Wyoming and your example of "What a Lawman's supposed to be", helped me put this book together. This one's for you brother.

Thank you

As always I am thankful for my Heavenly Father, God almighty for inspiring me and giving me the desires of my heart. Next I am thankful for my daughter Rebeccah and my wife Cheryl for helping me with proof reading and editing. Thank you Theresa Jackson for all your amazing editing help and Daniel Lee Salter of Great Britain for your copy editing and proof reading services. Writing this book was an amazing journey and I am thrilled to have such wonderful people help me do it.

Table of Contents

The
LEGEND
of
DEPUTY JIM

Sneak Peek:
Sheridan County
Sheriff's Department 1974

Jim is still upset over his encounter with the tourist guys in the souped-up VW van. He really could not put his finger on why they bugged him so much. When that blond-haired guy grabbed and kissed Linda's hand, he felt like ripping both their heads off. The last thing he needed right now was to lose his temper over something stupid and have Al pissed off at him. He pulls into the department parking lot, gets out, takes a calming breath, and walks in to talk to Al about what just went down in Cheyenne.

Standing by the reception desk just inside the door are Al and Manning, talking about the news from Cheyenne. Manning says, "All four are dead. How is that even possible?"

Al shakes his head, takes off his hat, and rubs his eyes. "George, all I know is that Michaels called me up around 4 a.m. to tell me that Reno, Sisko, and Belinda were murdered last night, and we already know that Arson was found dead in his cell at the beginning of the week. They figured out that Arson was poisoned with some crap from South America called 'Angel's Breath.' It puts you in a state of amnesia, and if you take too much, it kills you while you sleep. Belinda and the other two had their necks broken. She was raped before she died."

Sheriff Manning closes his eyes, drops his chin to his chest, and shakes his head solemnly. He looks up to see Jim coming through the front door. "Al, you and Jim join me in my office in thirty minutes. I am going to process this a while. Tell Lucy to hold all my calls until after we meet." He nods his head to Jim, then turns and walks to his office.

Prologue

The Rainbow Bar, Present Day, Sheridan, Wyoming

Major Joe Mason of the Wyoming Highway Patrol sits at the bar that his nephew Bill has managed for the last twenty-some years and enjoys his Friday night brewskie before heading back to the ranch and calling it quits for the evening. Tonight was kind of special, because the grandson of one of Sheridan's finest lawmen was retiring from the coast guard and wanted to talk to him about getting onto the highway patrol.

Joe has been with the highway patrol for almost fifty years now and can't remember a better man than Lieutenant Al Freeburger of the Sheridan County Sheriff's Department. Al shut his eyes for the last time fifteen years ago. He was survived by one daughter, Pearl, who married one of the Schuette boys. Joe looks up and sees Marvin Schuette walk through the door from Main Street. He gives him a smile, and waves him over to the bar.

Marv has a medium build with dark, leathery skin and the easy stride of a man who has spent much of his life on the ocean. He quickly makes his way to the old highway patrolman. "Joe, thanks for taking the time. I really appreciate it," Marvin says as he vigorously shakes his hand and takes a seat on the stool in front of the famous Rainbow Bar counter.

Bill Mason walks over from behind the counter and gives him a half-smile. "Looky what we have here, another wayward child come back to the nest. I know you been away for a while now,

Marv. How about I get you something nice and light, like a virgin Shirley Temple?"

Marvin just laughs and grabs his old friend's extended hand. "Uh, waitress, I'll have a CLC and Coke, and skip the cherry."

Bill grins from ear to ear. "You Schuettes sure can be assholes. Welcome home, buddy." All three laugh as Bill turns around to make Marvin's drink.

As both men settle in, Joe turns to face Marvin. "So, after twenty years in the coast guard patrolling the Caribbean in those big Hamilton and National Security cutters, you want to come home to drive a little squad car and catch speeders, huh? Seeing who your grandpa was, I thought for sure you'd go talk to the sheriff and get on with him."

Marvin grabs his drink from Bill. "You know, that was the first thing I looked into, but there are no real openings coming up until next year. Plus, the state has better pay, benefits, and retirement than the county."

As they are talking, Bill walks back over and puts a *Sheridan Tribune* newspaper in front of both men and points out the lead story. On the front page is a picture of a familiar family standing in front of a Pennsylvania automobile dealership, and the headline says, "The Hero of Cozumel Alive and Well. Jim Edwards Family Safe and Sound."

Bill looks at Marvin and asks, "Didn't you say Commander Jacob Edwards was your commanding officer for a while?"

With obvious pride, Marv looks at both men. "Not only was he the best commanding officer I ever served under, I was with him at Cozumel that day. Hell, I'm the one who fired the OTO Melara 76 mm at the attacking pirate cutter and covered him when sniper fire came our way."

Joe takes the newspaper away from Marvin and looks at the picture of Jim's whole family. He thinks to himself that Linda is as beautiful as ever, and can't help but recognize how her grand-daughter, Danielle, favors her in a lot of ways. He laughs for a moment, lost in thoughts of days gone by, and looks up. "Yup, Little Chunk grew up and did his daddy proud. That apple didn't fall far from the tree. Those two are a couple of peas in a pod."

Marvin looks over at Joe. "Yeah, I heard the commander is every bit as good a businessman as his dad. I guess he's running the whole operation now."

Joe drops the newspaper on the counter, sits straight up, looks at Marvin and Bill, and gives a huff. "Businessman, huh? Anybody that can work hard, do some math, and control them-selves can make a buck or two. Didn't your grandpa ever talk to you about Jim Edwards?"

Under Joe's glare, Marvin nervously squirms in his seat. "Gramps never talked much about the sheriff's department or the Marine Corps. Mom did tell me Jim was a deputy for a few years, but he didn't have the right temperament for the job. I asked the commander about it once, and he just said his mom and dad refused to tell him much about those days. Why?"

Joe lets out a breath, sits back, and smiles. "Yes, I remember that. I was standing right there on their porch in Story after Jim took down the rest of those bikers. That's when Linda made him promise never to talk with Jacob about what went on. Looks like he kept his promise."

Bill leans across the bar and says, "I remember when I first started working here and heard you and Al in here talking about that stuff with the bikers up in Story in the early '70s. That was Jim Edwards, huh?"

Joe tells Bill to get them both another drink as he settles back in his stool and affectionately looks at these two men who are about half his age. "Boys, the whole damn world knows about the hero of Cozumel, but I'm going to tell you about the legend of Deputy Jim."

Chapter One
Little About Jim

1972, Sheridan, Wyoming

They didn't call them smokers for nothing. Somehow, even when held in a school gym, all the old cowboys felt like it was their constitutional right to smoke their cigars as they watched all the boys beat the hell out of each other for three rounds. The gymnasium of Sheridan Central Middle School was not Madison Square Garden, but it was where all the best boxing "smokers" took place on Saturday afternoons in that part of northern Wyoming. The school district allowed it because most of the revenue from the ticket sales, plus all the concessions profit for the day, went straight to them.

That never stopped Dr. Caroline Lard, the school principal, from making an appearance at the next PTA meeting to complain. She always had to open up all the doors and windows in that part of the school to air it out all weekend. On Mondays, teachers and students alike would say that they could still smell the "smokers' ghost" from the Saturday matches.

The next to the last fight is winding down as Jim Edwards readies himself in the back by the dressing rooms. Being twenty-one, he fought in the over-eighteen heavyweight men's category. He had a good couple of years in this circuit, and he was billed as the main event for the last couple of smokers he was in.

Today is different. Today, he faces the state champion, Richard Ladenza, from Powell, Wyoming. Richard is a power puncher to the nth degree. Knockouts are not common in AAU (American Athletic Union) amateur sponsored boxing. All participants are required to wear headgear, and the rules of the contest are designed to keep the participants from getting injured. But Richard has five knockouts to his credit. In their last match, he knocked Jim down several times, broke his nose, and almost earned a TKO. That was four months ago, and Jim is ready for some payback.

Jim stands six feet two inches tall and weighs 210 pounds. His opponent is his physical equal. Jim has speed, good power, and an iron jaw. Richard has two sledgehammers he calls fists. Jim eyes Richard on the other side of the ring, hoping his new strategy will pay off. While deep in thought, he feels a tiny hand on his glove and he looks down to see his three-year-old son, Jacob, tugging on him to lift him up. He imploringly looks over at Linda, his wife, who just rolls her eyes. "You're the one who wanted us both here."

Jim then reaches down and picks up his "little chunk." He calls him that because at three years old, the kid felt like solid muscle. Jacob is curious about everything, and he starts to pull at his father's headgear, mouthpiece, and gloves. Despite himself, Jim starts to poke his son in the belly with his gloved thumb, and Jacob screams with laughter. He almost misses being called to the match, but his coach comes up and slaps the back of his head. He quickly hands Jacob back to Linda and climbs up into the ring.

This is his hometown, and there are a lot of cheers, whoops, and hollers as he steps to the middle of the ring and waves. The last time he faced Richard was in Powell, and everyone booed him. When Richard steps in, though, there is no booing for the state champion in the Sheridan crowd, just a hushed silence and an unmistakable show of respect. Everyone hopes that Jim can do better this time against the "Powell Brawler," as they call him, but they are also excited because of the rumors that Richard is going to the semi-finals for a spot on the Olympic Boxing Team, and that's a feather in Wyoming's athletic cap that everyone wants.

Both men step to the center of the ring as the referee, who is also a local real estate auctioneer named Sam Mason, greets them and quickly goes over the rules. Sam looks directly at Richard. "If your opponent is going down, you don't keep beating him down. When I say 'step away,' you do it or I will disqualify you, state champion or not." Both men touch gloves and turn to their respective corners. Jim is thinking, *thanks for the vote of confidence, Sam.*

The tension in the room is as thick as the cigar smoke, and a couple of fans are set up to help blow the worst of the latter outside, so the two fighters can breathe and see. The bell rings, and the fighters catapult themselves to the center of the ring. As usual, Richard starts pounding on his opponent's arms, endeavoring to get through to the head. His strategy has always been simple and direct—pummel until the opponent's guard drops, then beat on him until the fight is stopped or the man goes down. This time, Jim is ready for Richard and lunges low. He comes up under Richard's assault and begins one of his own to the champ's midsection. He doesn't care about power just yet—all he wants to do is freak out his opponent with how many shots he can get into his gut.

Jim has always been fast, but something is turbocharging his engine this time, and his gloves are slapping against Richard's ribs and abdomen at light speed, as he pushes the state champion back into the corner. He continues his attack to the body but starts to add some head shots. Richard is no slouch and manages to get in some good shots of his own as they basically finish the round in the corner. When the bell rings, everyone knows that

Jim Edwards just pulled off the impossible and took the first round away from Richard Ladenza.

As sweet as the victory is, it is short-lived. Richard comes out like a bull in the second round and pushes Jim around the ring for three long minutes, pummeling him with one devastating blow after another. Jim survives, if only barely.

To some, six minutes of boxing might not seem like much, but to an amateur fighter, it's an eternity. Both men come out for the third and final round, looking like they would rather just go home. But to their credit, when the bell rings they fight and give it everything they have. At times, it looks like Richard is going to knock Jim out, and at other times it seems that Jim is keeping him tied up in a corner. During the last minute of the fight, Jim changes his strategy and starts fighting in the middle of the ring. Richard tries to attack with power but Jim ducks, jabs, and moves. He even gets in a couple of good flurries to the face before the final bell rings.

It takes the judges forever to score the cards. It even looks like a couple of them get in an argument, but Sam tells them to knock it off. He grabs the cards and brings them to the center of the ring. He calls Jim and Richard in to meet him. He looks at both young men. "Folks, we have a tie." He raises both men's arms up and then pats them on the back and exits the ring.

Jim and Richard stay in the ring and look at each other for a second, then Richard extends his ungloved hand. "You're better than I thought, Edwards. You still quitting after this one?"

Jim reaches out and takes Richard's hand. "You're damn right. I'm not doing that again. I start my new job at the sheriff's department next week after I graduate. Linda says being a deputy is dangerous enough. You go get 'em at the Olympic trials. We're all rooting for you." With that, they hug, and then Jim raises Richard's hand in the air, points at him, and gives a thumbs-up. Everyone cheers and they both exit the ring.

Jim gets down and walks over to Linda and Jacob. Every time he looks at his family, he can't believe what a lucky guy he is. Linda and her mom moved to Sheridan right after her father died in Vietnam as a navy pilot. Her mother had been a school teacher in New England but was offered a job as the principal of Coffeen Elementary School by the Sheridan County school board.

Jim first met Linda at Woodland Park Middle School because her mother chose to live in Story, Wyoming, which was about fifteen miles south of Sheridan, nestled in the Bighorn Mountains. Story had a grade school, but no middle or high school, so the children were bussed down to Woodland Park, the closest middle school to Story, and later to Sheridan High School. From then until their junior year in high school, Jim spent the time working up the courage to ask her out. Being a beautiful girl from the East Coast made Linda quite popular in Sheridan County.

It seemed every time he thought he might ask her out, he'd find that one of the other guys had beat him to it. Finally, during the summer between their junior and senior year, she was working as a waitress at the same place he worked as a line cook. They had always been friends but nothing more. While sitting at the coffee bar at the end of their shifts, he finally just did it and asked her out. When she said yes, he was stunned.

She laughed and punched him in the shoulder. "I've been waiting years for you to work up the courage, dummy. Sometimes I think you've got brain damage from all that boxing you're doing."

After that day, Jim and Linda were inseparable. They both turned eighteen during their senior year and snuck off to Nevada one weekend during Christmas break and got married. They tried to keep it quiet for the rest of the year, but when Linda's baby bump started to show, they had to announce to their family and friends that they were married.

He looks at her now and can't believe what a lucky guy he is. She is so beautiful, and Jacob is everything he ever dreamed a son could be.

He walks up, kisses Linda, and goes to pick up Jacob, but she stops him and orders him to the shower. Jacob grabs his daddy's leg anyway and says he wants to go with him, but Linda isn't hearing that at all. She grabs him and tells Jim to meet them out at the truck in the parking lot.

Thirty minutes later, Jim meets Jacob and Linda by his 1958 International pickup truck that he just finished restoring at the Sheridan Community College auto body technical school. He didn't major in auto bodywork, but he did take a couple of classes while he worked on his associate degree in criminal justice. He always loved working on cars and trucks, and they needed another vehicle. Money was very tight, so he found the International in front of an old barn out on Highway 90 and picked it up for thirty-five dollars. It was just a matter of getting it to run, which he and his dad did out in front of his parent's place. Once they got it running, he took it to the college and offered it as a project for the auto-body class. They accepted it, and he enrolled in the class so that he could work on it and be a part of the whole restoration process.

The bodywork was very good, and the truck looked like it did when it was new. Jim never could bring himself to change the look of a vehicle. Someone told him that when you changed the factory look, it brought the resale price down, and it could never be sold as an antique. All of his buddies tried to talk him into mag wheels and flames, but he refused. When it rolled out of the college body shop, the used-car manager at Sheridan Autos was there and offered him one thousand dollars for it. He almost took the money but decided to keep the truck because Linda and Jacob liked it a lot.

As he walks up to his family, Linda smiles. "You better be gawking at me and not this stupid truck, or you'll be sleeping in it tonight."

Jim laughs as he grabs his wife and kisses her, then looks at Jacob. "Rule number one, Little Chunk—Mommy is first, then you and me, then the truck." Jacob rolls his eyes and starts to pound on the door for his daddy to open it. Inside, a three-month-old Siberian Husky Malamute mixed-breed puppy starts yelping his brains out.

Linda bends down and helps Jacob inside to sit with his new puppy, Thunder, whom they had just gotten for Jacob's birthday. Once Jacob is settled in, Linda reaches up, cups Jim's cheek in the palm of her hand and looks at her husband's face. "Well, at least Richard was kind enough not to give you a couple of black eyes on your graduation day." The couple hop in the truck and head up the mountain to Story.

After he got married, Jim kept his job at the Sheridan Center Inn as a cook so that he could save money for school. They chose to live in Story with Linda's mom, who loved helping take care of the baby. After one year and with both their parents' help, he was able to take night and weekend classes at the college. He decided on law enforcement, because he always thought he would enlist in the military some day after he graduated from high school. But with getting married and having a baby right away, he could not do that to his family. So, he decided the best way he could serve his country was to become a lawman and protect his friends and neighbors.

Jim's graduation ceremony is at seven o'clock that night and the smoker got over at noon. It is a little less than a thirty-minute drive to Story, where they would all get ready and then head back to Sheridan. About three-quarters of the way up the mountain they run into a traffic jam, which in that area could mean a few things, like construction, an accident, or a police pullover.

Jim pulls up behind the line of stopped vehicles. At this place on the mountain, the road is so windy that he cannot see more than a couple of cars ahead. He decides to get out and walk around the bend to see what's going on. Once he's within eyeshot of the problem, the hair on the back of his neck pops up and his adrenaline starts to flow. He turns around and runs back to his truck. He reaches behind the seat and pulls out his dad's old pump shotgun, puts three rounds in, chambers one, and inserts another. He nervously looks at his wife. "Take Jacob and go back to town. Sheriff Manning has a bunch of biker gang boys pulled over and it looks like he's in trouble. They don't have the repeater set up in Story yet, so he doesn't have any way of radioing his deputies. I'm going to try and help him."

Linda knows that Jim is going to be doing this for a living from now on and cannot think of an objection that will work, so she just gets in the driver's seat, kisses her husband, and turns the truck around to race back to Sheridan to get some help.

As Jim passes each car in the traffic jam on the mountain road, he tells the driver what's going on around the corner and says to turn around and get out of there. They all obey, but when he gets to the vehicle closest to the incident, he sees that it's empty. A cold chill goes down his spine when he realizes what's going on. The bikers are using some people as hostages to keep Sheriff Manning from acting.

The winding pass that they are all on is bordered by a guard-rail on one side that looks out over the Sheridan Valley below and the sheer, rocky wall of the mountain on the other side. He crosses the highway to the side with the mountain wall and stealthily makes his way around the corner. He sees the sheriff facing two big bikers whose backs are to him. To the side are three more bikers holding a couple at knifepoint. He hears one of the bikers tell the sheriff that if he doesn't let them leave, he'll have his boys slit the girl's throat and throw her off the side of the mountain. Behind the group and closest to the couple being held hostage are five Harley Davidson choppers.

No one has seen Jim yet, so he slowly backs up and goes over to the couple's car which is abandoned around the corner, out of eyeshot from the group. He sighs with relief as he notices that the car is an automatic, and the keys are still in the ignition. Jim gets in, starts the engine, maneuvers the steering wheel so that the car will go straight at the five Harleys, puts it in gear, and opens the door. He steps on the gas and rolls out of the car at the same time. The little Ford Falcon gains just enough momentum to smash into the five bikes, doing considerable damage to the first two.

Nothing pisses a biker off more than having his pride and joy messed with. All five of them forget what they are doing and run to their bikes. Jim sees that the hostages and Sheriff Manning are free, so he steps around the corner and unloads two shotgun shells into one of the bikes that didn't get much damage from the Falcon. He then points his shotgun at the obvious leader. "You boys better just get down on your knees and put your hands up on top of your heads or this henhouse is going to be minus one rooster real quick."

Sheriff Manning is able to retrieve his firearm from one of the bikers, and he walks over to Jim. "Jim, you don't even start till next week, so if you don't mind, I'll handle arresting these assholes. Just go over to my squad car and get some extra cuffs. And thanks, kid. That was getting pretty hairy, and you did some quick thinking."

The leader sneers and spits on the ground as the sheriff is cuffing him. He looks Jim in the eye. "You best watch your ass, cowshit. You and I have a score to settle later."

Sheriff Manning comes up and puts his hand on Jim's shoulder. "The only thing this jerk is going to settle is whether he gets playtime in the prison yard or not."

As Jim and the sheriff are getting the prisoners situated against the highway guardrail, two sheriff patrol cars and one highway patrol cruiser come around the corner with their lights flashing. Behind them, about fifty yards back, Linda is sitting in the International with Jacob, praying that Jim is all right. Once the rest of the commissioned law enforcement officers get out to help the sheriff, Jim grabs his dad's shotgun and walks back to his wife and son.

As soon as she sees Jim come around the corner, Linda grabs Jacob and runs up to him, throws herself into his arms, and starts to cry. "You sure you want to do this for a living? You about scared ten years out of me when you pulled that stunt."

He holds her for a few moments, grabs his son, and gently walks the two back to his truck. When he gets in, Thunder jumps on his lap and starts licking him from ear to ear.

Jim and Linda do make it to his graduation ceremony, along with practically the whole sheriff's department and a couple of Wyoming highway patrolmen. When it comes time to recognize the five criminal justice graduates, Sheriff Manning steps up to the podium and tells the whole crowd about the incident at Story earlier that day. When Jim goes up to get his diploma, the sheriff hands it to him while the whole auditorium at Sheridan Community College gives him a standing ovation.

Chapter Two
Deputized

One Week Later, Sheridan County Sheriff's Department

Jim can't believe this day is finally here. Ever since he decided to go into law enforcement, he debated on which department to try for. The deciding factor was that Sheriff Manning and his dad were old high school buddies. His dad, Carl Edwards, was a dyed-in-the-wool railroad man who had worked for Burlington Northern Railways. Jim could never see himself doing that for a living, but he sure respected his old man's commitment to railroad tradition. The sheriff told Carl that if Jim were to show that he was serious and get a degree in criminal justice, he'd give the kid a shot. Of course, he also had to complete the Wyoming Law Enforcement Academy's basic peace officer training course, which he did the previous summer.

Jim is standing next to two senior deputies in front of Sheriff Manning. Jim is already in uniform, and Manning has him raise his right hand and repeat the oath. When he's finished, the sheriff hands him his badge and his new Taurus .357 duty pistol, shakes his hand, and welcomes him to the department.

The sheriff points to the older deputy on Jim's right. "Jim, this is Lieutenant Al Freeburger. He'll be your trainer and immediate superior. Okay, boys, get out of my office and go get some work done."

With that, the three leave, and Jim follows Al to the break room.

Al looks at Jim admiring his new firearm. "You know, you have to pay for that. It's two hundred and seventy-five dollars. The sheriff will take ten bucks a week out of your check until it's paid off. If you quit or are fired before your last payment, he'll take what you owe out of your last paycheck. If that's not enough, you'll be billed for the rest."

"What if I want to pay it off sooner? Will the sheriff let me do that?" Jim asks.

Al laughs. "Kid, if you got two hundred and seventy-five bucks to throw away, be my guest. Just go down to the finance office and talk to Lucy."

Jim makes like he is going, but Al stops him and tells him they have a few more details to go over before he can do that. A couple hours later, and with his head spinning from all the information Al just imparted, he walks into the sheriff's finance office and meets a middle-age, heavyset woman named Lucy. "Howdy, ma'am. My name is Jim Edwards, and I want to talk about my duty pistol payments."

Lucy looks up over her horn-rimmed glasses. "I'm sorry, Jim, but ten dollars a week is the lowest payment Sheriff Manning will take for a duty pistol payment."

Jim enthusiastically approaches her desk. "Yes, I understand, but what if I want to increase my payments?"

Lucy is taken aback by the request. "I've been here for over twenty years, and I swear that you're the very first person to ask me that." She takes her glasses off, sets them on her desk, and leans back. "I really don't see why we can't increase your payments. I'll just have to figure out a way to tell the sheriff so that it doesn't put him in cardiac arrest. What did you have in mind?"

"Well, ma'am, my wife and I have been living on one hundred and twenty-five dollars a week for the last three years from what I made at the Sheridan Center Inn as a line cook. I figure my check here will be somewhere between two fifty and two seventy-five a week, depending on overtime. So, I'd like to make two payments of $137.50 for the next two weeks. Would that be okay?"

Lucy leans forward, puts her glasses back on, and stares at Jim. "My God, George is going to have a heart attack when he hears this. But, yes, that is your privilege. I will put a note on your payroll account to do just that." Jim thanks her enthusiastically and leaves the office.

When Sheriff Manning gets the news of how Jim wants to handle paying off his duty pistol, he's shocked. Then, after thinking about it, he calls Al Freeburger and tells him to make sure that Jim gets at least ten hours of overtime every week until further notice.

One of the first things that Jim does with his new duty pistol is to take Linda out to the shooting range up by the fairgrounds off Fifth Street in Sheridan. She told him she always wanted to learn how to shoot, but the only gun Jim ever had to show her was his dad's old shotgun—the one he used to help Sheriff Manning out with the biker gang. They only went twice, because firing that cannon made her shoulder sore. A Taurus .357 revolver had quite a kick to it as well, but nothing compared to a shotgun.

As they pull into the shooting range area, they wave at Al Freeburger who is there to help out. Al figures it's good for a deputy's wife to know a little about the firearms in the house and should be competent at handling them. He really didn't mind letting Linda use his older .357 because he loved his new Colt Python, and his old Taurus just sat in his gun cabinet collecting dust.

Today, he is going to kill two birds with one stone, because Jim still needs to qualify with his duty pistol in front of a certified law-enforcement instructor to lawfully carry. Sheridan College did put Jim through a semester of firearms training for his criminal justice degree, but Jim's marks weren't great. He was left-eye dominant, which made his pistol craft a little too low, but his scores with the shotgun were the best Al had ever seen.

Al is the top marksman in the Rocky Mountain region for law enforcement. Not only has he won contests all over Wyoming, Montana, Idaho, and Colorado for sharp-shooting with his .357 duty pistol, but he was considered the fastest draw and re-loader as well. He had some ideas on how to get Jim's marks up for his aim, and he was going to use Linda to do it.

"Jim and Linda, nice to see you. Jim, get all your gear over here and we'll get set up. I have to be back on patrol in about two hours, so I'm going to put both of you through the instruction and qualification. Linda, that way you get to fire that bad boy two hundred times and Jim can get his requirements in too. Oh, and if you get the minimum score, you can qualify to carry for Wyoming state law enforcement."

Jim wraps his arm around Linda's shoulders and says with a chuckle, "You hear that, honey? Maybe you could be my patrol partner, huh?"

Al smirks. "I was talking to you about the qualification, kid. But yes, if Linda here scores high enough, I'll give her a certificate too."

Ten minutes later, Jim and Linda are standing in front of a couple of tables set up with two .357 revolvers and about five hundred rounds of ammunition. They listen as Al goes over all the rules and last-minute instructions. The first part of the test is stationary shooting and reloading. Ten yards back from the first set of targets, they are to fire and reload ten times. The targets are full-body figures on sheets that are three and a half feet long and two and a half feet wide. The requirement is to hit the center mass or head region on at least 75% of the shots. They strap on the holsters, put on their ear and eye protection, holster the weapons, and wait for Al to give the go-ahead.

Al says go, and they draw and commence firing. Jim notices that he is much faster than Linda at shooting and reloading. When she finishes her last load and fires her sixtieth round, Al tells both of them to stop. They holster their guns, and he walks up to inspect the targets. He writes something down on a clipboard, then turns around and says, "Jim, congratulations. You scored seventy-four percent. That's three percentage points up from your best score at college, but not good enough to pass yet. Linda, you got ninety-one percent. Nice shooting, honey."

Jim is dumbfounded that his wife did so much better than him. He looks imploringly at Al, who just laughs. "Take your time, kid. Aim small and miss small. Pay attention to your stance. Remember your training. You would not believe how many amateurs get into gunfights not ten yards away from one another, unload all their ammo and find that they did not hit a damn thing. Bullets are not free. Any one of them can save or take a life. Spend them like you spend money. I know you're careful with that stuff."

Jim takes Al's advice to heart. He concentrates on his stance, his breathing, and his form. The idea of treating each bullet like it is money communicated to him, and he starts spending them more thriftily. For the next hour, Jim and Linda go through a series of drills, like drawing their weapons, firing twice and holstering, walking a path and shooting a target upon command. When he's done, Jim has increased his score and ends up with 84 percent. Linda, however, really started getting the hang of it and finishes with 98 percent.

The next test Jim does by himself. It's a simple shotgun exercise. He has to expend twenty-one rounds in a walking and shooting exercise, reload twice, and get 80 percent or better and be done in ten minutes. He gets 100 percent and is done in five.

As they are packing up, Jim and Linda walk back over to Al's cruiser to thank him for doing the test and letting Linda join in. He is just finishing up with the certificates as he turns around and says, "You know, the sheriff didn't think I could even get more than a seventy-five out of you, kid. You see, he's left-eye dominant too. Best he's done in the twenty years I've known him is an eighty-six. That's why I was okay with you bringing Linda along. It was kind of a long shot, but over the years I've found that if a woman is not intimidated by a pistol, she usually does a little better than a man. It has something to do with how their arms have a slight bow in them that ours don't have—makes them hold it steadier. Now, a man can compensate by having a stronger grip and more mass to steady his aim, but he has to concentrate on his technique, which you started doing after you saw how badly your wife was kicking your ass. Be that as it may, Linda, you're a natural with a handgun. You ever want to go Annie Oakley and enter some contest, I'd love to coach you."

Linda smiles, walks over and kisses Al's cheek. "Thanks, Al, but I doubt I'll ever pick up one of those things again." She then rubs her hands together and massages her shoulder. "Two hundred rounds are quite enough for this girl. I'm going home now to get a soak in a hot tub and then Jim can give me a nice foot massage."

Al winks at Linda, then looks over in Jim's direction. "See you tomorrow, deputy. Don't forget to bring your firearm." They say goodbye and drive away from the shooting range. When the couple get home, Jim finds a frame and hangs his certificate in the living room. Linda gets a scrapbook out of one of her storage trunks, puts her certificate in it, and stores it away.

With Jim graduating from junior college at the end of the summer of 1972, he began his career as a sheriff's deputy that fall. Sheridan County, Wyoming encompasses 2,527 square miles and has a population of just over 21,000. Outside of Sheridan, the other major towns in the county are Ranchester, Dayton, Clearmont, Big Horn, and Story. Manning had only eight deputies to cover all that territory. Now Sheridan has its own police department and so does Ranchester, but everyone else depends on the sheriff's department and highway patrol to cover them.

After his first three months of riding along with Al Freeburger and covering the largest of the territories of Big Horn, Freemont, Banner, and Story, Jim is allocated the latter two as his territory. The sheriff and Freeburger decide that since Jim lives in Story, he should have that town in his patrol territory.

Al turns out to be an excellent tutor. He was a thirty-year Marine Corps veteran, and after having served in World War II, Korea, and Vietnam, he retired from the corps about ten years back as a sergeant major E9, the highest designation for a non-commissioned officer in the United States military. He is now second-in-command of the sheriff's department, and top sergeant in the National Guard in Sheridan and all of Wyoming. During the three months that he got to patrol with the old war-horse, Jim swore he learned more about his country's last three wars than was even touched on in his history classes at Sheridan High School or college.

As far as learning about being a deputy, Al teaches Jim how to keep a cool head and a pleasant demeanor when dealing with people. "We don't provoke nothing, but if someone wants to start a fight, we'll damn sure finish it." From September to December, Jim learns how to patrol traffic, when to pull over a speeder, and when to scare them a little by showing up in their rearview mirror. He also learns how to handle domestic relations calls and how to decide when to give counsel and when to arrest someone, which usually involves a drunk husband using his wife as a punching bag.

On one occasion, they receive a call from dispatch to respond to a little trailer park south of Sheridan called Woodland Park Trailer Community. As they are getting ready to respond, Sheriff Manning gets on the radio and tells Jim and Freeburger to pick him up on the way out. Once Manning gets in the squad car, he tells Jim to stay in the car when they get to the scene and keep his eyes forward when driving back to town.

Jim pulls up to a ratty looking, single-wide trailer in the third row of the park. Freeburger and Manning go up to the door and enter without even knocking. Five minutes later, they come out with a large, muscular man in his late thirties, wearing nothing but his boxer shorts and a dirty white tank top. Jim immediately recognizes him as one of the guys that works as a grease monkey at Sheridan Autos downtown. His name is Bob Jones, and this isn't the first time the sheriff's department has been called out to keep him from beating his wife to death. But as Jim is about to learn, it's the last.

Freeburger opens up the rear door and throws Jones into the back seat. He gets in and sits next to him, and Sheriff Manning gets in on the other side. Jones has his hands cuffed behind his back, and he stares ahead at the back of Jim's head.

"You just take it nice and slow back to town, Jim. Me and Al want to have a heart-to-heart with old Bob here." When the ambulance came, Jim caught a good look at Bob's wife and could tell that he really gave her a good beating, so he is very interested in what the sheriff has in mind. He does not have to wait long to find out.

"Bob, I told you the next time I come out here and find Nancy like that, you're going to regret it. I guess you didn't believe me."

With that, Al sends an elbow into Bob's nose, breaking it. It is about eight miles back to Sheridan and the police department, which is where all the holding cells are. Every time Jim hits a bump or takes a turn, either the sheriff or Freeburger elbows, punches, or slams Bob's face into the front seat and the chicken wire mesh that separates the cab. By the time they pull up to the jail entrance, Bob looks as bad, if not worse, than his wife.

As Sheriff Manning is signing him in to the Sheridan PD, the duty sergeant asks what the hell happened to Bob. Manning just smiles. "Damnedest thing, Sarge, but this time Nancy got ahold of a frying pan and fought back. Then when we got there, he tried resisting arrest. I guess his little winter stay in the county jail ain't going to be so pleasant this time."

The duty sergeant looks at Bob and asks him if that's what happened. While looking at the ground, Bob shakes his head. "Yes. I got drunk with some friends, came home and there was nothing to eat, so I slapped Nancy a couple of times, and she grabbed the pan and says I can eat it and starts hitting me with it. The neighbors called you guys and I panicked. I'm sorry."

The sergeant is writing all this down. He's no idiot and pretty much figured out what really happened, but he's also 100 percent behind the sheriff and just says thanks, they'll handle it from here.

When Sheriff Manning and Freeburger get back in the squad car, the sheriff looks at Jim and says, "Don't ever talk about this. Okay, son?"

Jim grows a big grin on his face and says, "My dad always says you're the best damn sheriff we've ever had, and you just proved that to me tonight, boss." He then takes his fingers and pulls them across his lips, mimicking pulling shut a zipper.

Manning smiles and looks at Freeburger. "I like this kid. Maybe some of us old farts can look forward to retirement after all, huh?"

Freeburger smiles back. "I hear you there, George. You find three or four more like him and I'll make that biker gang problem we've been talking about ancient history."

Jim doesn't quite get what Al is talking about, but he's glad that his boss knows he is all for making wife-beaters know they won't get away with it. As for the biker problem, he can only guess.

It was the middle of December when the incident with Bob and Linda Jones occurred. Not much happened the rest of the winter of '72–'73. During the following summer, Jim got a good education regarding what it was like to be a full-blown Sheridan County sheriff's deputy. Working mostly with Freeburger, he wrote more traffic citations than he could count. He also chased down and arrested three separate bank robbers, cleaned up a drug-smuggling ring trying to form in Banner, and spent a considerable amount of time chasing after renegade biker gangs harassing people around Story and Banner.

Although Jim did not compete in amateur boxing anymore, he still liked to exercise as much as he did. He had a heavy bag and a speed bag hanging out in the garage. In the winter, there was a potbelly wood stove that he stoked up before his workouts. After Thunder turned a year old, he was big enough to go on runs with Jim. Jim usually ran three to five miles after a thirty-minute bag workout. Thunder loved to run, so much so that Jim would make his way to a big meadow on the edge of Story where he would cut the dog loose while he ran around it. The meadow was about three-quarters of a mile in diameter and Jim would lap it once or twice, depending on how excited the dog was to be out in the middle of it.

He loved to see Thunder run. The dog was ninety pounds now, with a sleek black and white coat and brown eyes. Jim swore he looked like a racehorse when he took off. The way that dog glided through the air was something to behold, and it always made Jim want to run harder. Thunder is a real snow dog, so in the winter when Jim had to stick to the road on his run, he still cut Thunder loose in that meadow and just stopped and watched him tear through the drifts like they were there for his private pleasure.

In addition to Jim keeping up on his boxing conditioning, he was always invited to the weekly physical training sessions Al did with his guardsmen. Jim got a taste of what it was like to go through a little Marine Corps-style hand-to-hand combat training. He really liked it, especially the judo.

Chapter Three
Temper, Temper

Fall of 1973

The gang that was involved in the highway incident with Sheriff Manning and Jim the previous year was called "The Wild Wolves." Like their name suggests, they were a pack of ravenous beasts who had long memories and little self-control. Among the five who were arrested that day was Todd Belking, aka Grinder. He was the number two man in the gang, and the leader who Jim threatened to take out with his dad's shotgun on the highway that day. Because of some technicalities concerning Jim's involvement in the arrest while not being a commissioned peace officer, Belking's lawyer negotiated a plea bargain that got him a reduced sentence in the Sheridan County jail. In October of '73 he was released. Sheriff Manning, Jim, and Al Freeburger were all there when his gang members came to pick him up.

Like most of the guys in his gang, Todd was ex-military, dishonorably discharged from the marines back in '68 for insubordination. He stood six feet two inches and weighed just under 250. He had heavily muscled arms covered with tattoos and a bushy, blond beard and mustache.

When Grinder steps out of the building, he looks at the others waiting for him with his chopper sitting out front, all cleaned up and ready for its rider. He throws his head back and gives out a big howl like a wolf, and the rest respond in kind. As he is walking to the steps, he spots Jim and recognizes him. He gives a big huff, throws his shoulders back, walks over to where he is standing, and sticks his mouth right up to Jim's ear. "Now don't you look all cute and cuddly in that new Boy Scout sheriff's outfit. My boys tell me you have a pretty little hot thing waiting for you at home. Maybe I'll have to go pay her a visit some time, show her what a real man feels like. Then I'll throw her over that guardrail down the side of the mountain off the road up there. What do you say, cowshit?"

Jim has long fuses for just about anything, but threatening his wife or child isn't one of them. He feels the blood rush to his head and start to pulse behind his eyeballs, and his hands and arms start to shake. His teeth begin to chatter a little as he pushes Grinder back and pops him in the face with a fast straight-arm left jab. Grinder lets out a roar and tries to haul back and knock Jim's head off, but Jim is way too quick and begins to pummel Grinder with a barrage of fists so fast and hard that he can't even get his guard up, nor can he stop from being beaten down the stairs and straight onto his chopper, which he knocks over as he falls against it.

But before Jim can jump on Grinder, he feels two steel hands grab his shoulders from behind and throw him like a rag doll to the side. Where Jim was standing seconds ago, Freeburger is now. He reaches down and quick-draws his .357 duty pistol and points it at Grinder. "Now, I think that the head dog here ought to learn himself how to walk down some steps like a grownup. I'm sure you can all agree that the sheriff is being mighty merciful in not putting him back in jail for threatening one of his deputies, can't we?"

Jim is starting to settle down a little but is mad enough to say, "I'll see that biker bastard pushing up daisies before he ever threatens me or mine again."

Al looks over at Jim with an understanding eye that comes from serving in three wars and ten years on the force. He winks and smiles. That tells Jim he knows exactly how he feels.

Al then looks back up at the sheriff who simply nods his head. He turns back to the five bikers. "Grinder, if you're anywhere within two hundred miles of Sheridan within the next six hours, my highway patrol buddies will take you and your girlfriends there to the state pen in Rawlins. You know what happens then. Now get."

Grinder's four buddies help him pick his bike up and let him kick-start it. He sits there for a few seconds, waiting for his men to get their bikes going. He has too much pride to wipe the blood away from his mouth and eyes as he turns and says, "Pack Leader ain't goin' to like this, Manning." With that, he turns his chopper around and leaves with the rest of his boys following.

After they leave, Al gets on the radio with the Sheridan PD and the highway patrol to make sure that Grinder and his boys are seen leaving Wyoming. Sheriff Manning walks down the stairs and over to where Jim is now standing. Jim is very nervous about what his boss is going to say, so he stands there fully ready for a good balling out. To his astonishment, the sheriff just smiles, laughs, and pats him on the back. "I ain't never even heard of anyone beating the hell out of Grinder like that before. Hell, Jim, he didn't have a chance. If you fought like that in the ring, we'd be sending you to the Olympics next year and not that Rocky Marciano wannabe from Powell."

Manning walks back to his car to head back to the sheriff's department. Al gets done with his radio calls and motions Jim over to him. "How about you and me grabbing a bite to eat at Brown's Drug Store Diner and having a little talk?"

They head over to Main Street downtown, park in the lot behind the Bank of Commerce next to the bowling alley and walk over to the diner. For about an hour, Al asks Jim a myriad of questions about his past, his dad, and his whole family, mainly concerning violence and tempers.

Jim tells him that there were very few episodes in his past where he really got mad like he did today. He remembers one time when he was about nine years old and some older boys shot his dog with a BB gun. He chased them down and tackled the one with the gun and was going to bash his head in when he felt someone grab him and pull him off. That someone was his dad, and he told Jim that if he ever lost his temper like that again, he was going to find out what kind of temper his dad had.

That was when his dad signed him up for the local boxing team. He told his son that he had to learn how to control his temper in intense situations and being in the ring with all its rules was a good place to start. The coach was a good friend of the family and took a special interest in Jim to teach him how to maintain ice-cold control while in the ring.

"After that, I really tried to not let things upset me, but no one ever threatened Linda like that before." He takes a deep, calming breath and continues. "I won't let anyone do it again either. If it means my job, then so be it."

Al sits there and stares at Jim with an unreadable look in his eyes. The tension at the table is uncomfortable, but Jim is guessing that Al is a lot more worried than mad. So, he just asks, "What's up, Lieutenant? Am I all wrong for the job or something?"

Al sits back and lets out a big puff of air, then takes his hands and rubs his temples. "You know, kid, I've been in three wars now. After the marines made me retire, I joined the sheriff's department, and I've been with George for ten years. I've seen a lot. I can spot a glory hound a mile away, and I know a hothead when I see them too. You ain't either one."

Jim sighs a breath of relief when Al says that, but before he can respond Al continues. "You're a hero, Jim, plain and simple." He then raises a hand. "But that ain't necessarily a good thing either. That means you tend to put everyone and everything before yourself. I don't just mean in everyday life. I am talking about when the shit hits the fan and all hell is breaking loose, you think you're the most expendable and everyone else matters first. Guys like you also tend to be something else that scares the hell out of me."

Jim sits up. "What's that?"

Al leans in and looks Jim in the eye. "You might be a berserker too."

"What the hell is that?" Jim asks, slumping back in his seat.

Al goes on to explain that a berserker is someone who in intense moments—combat especially—loses all awareness of self-preservation and throws himself into the battle with no other goal than destroying the enemy. Sometimes it's like they have superhuman abilities, because they have no hesitation in their actions. "I've seen this a few times in my life. I had a corporal once, nicest kid you ever want to meet. Pleasant, even-tempered, and competent as hell. But when the shit hit the fan and the enemy was coming in, he thought he was supposed to win the whole damn war himself. He couldn't stand to watch others risk their lives. He'd have to do that himself. In the South Pacific during the big one, the Japs had us pinned down right in the middle of a climb up a cliff. Before I knew what was going on, he rappelled back down to the beach, manned a .50 cal machinegun nest, and kept the enemy pinned down until we made it up to the top."

"What's wrong with that?" Jim responds. "Sounds like he made a logical decision that paid off in the end."

"Kid, there was a reason we didn't man that .50 cal. Anyone standing down there firing up was a sitting duck. All it would take was one sharpshooter off to the side to take him out. It was lucky for us that it took the Japs so long to get one of their guys over there. But the corporal never made it. It would have taken wild horses to pry his hands away from that machine gun. Later on, when we got back down, he was almost gone but was still holding on to that damn gun. Oh, sure, he got all kinds of medals and recognition after he died that day. But that wasn't much consolation for his mom and everybody else who loved him." Al leans forward. "When you were beating Grinder down those stairs, I saw that same look in your eyes."

Al takes another sip of his coffee and continues. "Last year, when you pulled that stunt helping the sheriff out on the road up to Story, it was foolish, reckless, heroic, and pretty damn crafty. I knew then that I had to keep my eye on you. Most guys would have just gone to get help, like you sent Linda to go and do. One out of a million would have gone in there by himself and confronted those boys. Then today with Grinder, no one has ever to my knowledge thrown him a beating like that. You were unstoppable. I knew I had to get to you from behind or you would have torn my head off. Grinder was scared shitless and in total shock. He's right—his boss, Pack Leader, ain't going to like this at all, and he's gonna have to do something to save face for himself and Grinder. There's a shit storm coming, kid, and you're going to be right in the middle of it."

Jim sits there trying to absorb everything Al is telling him, not quite sure how to respond. He finally just says, "Okay, Al, what does this mean for me?"

Al reaches over and lightly pounds his fist on the back of Jim's hand. "What this means, young man, is that I like you, and you have a beautiful wife and a wonderful son. So I'm going to keep a very close eye on you, and if it ever looks like you're going to get all sacrificial and shit with your life, I'll do everything in my power to take that badge away from you. You understand?"

Jim nods his head.

Al gets up. "Take the rest of the day off, kid. I'll cover your shift today. Go home and think about what I said. Remember, we're a team."

For the rest of the winter of '73–'74, Jim plays it cool, professional, and low key, but he still does his job very well.

South of Sierra Vista, Arizona, Biker Camp of the Wild Wolves on the Mexican Border

Bikers don't like the winter, especially the ones up north. Grinder always left around November and returned in the spring. Normally, he would leave a couple of boys up in Story to watch over business, but being run out of town after his one-year stay in the Sheridan County jail made it so that he had no clue what Seth, their pack leader, did about Story for the winter.

He pulls his bike around to the back of the camp and makes his way to the center to see if Seth aka Pack Leader is in the mood to talk.

Seth sees his wayward second-in-command tentatively make his way to him. He still can't believe that Todd got his ass kicked by a rookie deputy up in Sheridan. He thinks he's the only man who can do that, and it disturbs him how easily his second was throttled. One of the boys tries to tell him that Todd was probably just a little soft, having spent a year in a cell. But Pack Leader knows you don't get soft inside. For a biker, you have two choices—get hard or get dead. Grinder looks very much alive, and that means they both have a problem to deal with up in Story next spring.

But right now, he has to help Grinder save face in front of the whole pack. Grinder and Pack Leader could be twins except for the color of their hair. Where Grinder is a deep strawberry blond, Pack Leader has jet-black hair. Both men stand six feet two inches tall and weigh just under 250. Their arms and chest are heavily muscled and tattooed, both have somewhat of a beer belly, and they each have a couple of tree trunks for legs.

Each is ex-military, but where Grinder was kicked out of the marines for insubordination, Pack Leader was an honorably discharged captain from the Marine Corps Force Recon. Both men met in Nam in '66 and were in separate battalions. Unknown to the marines, they were in business together smuggling drugs out of the country and to the United States. When it looked like they were going to get caught, Grinder disobeyed a superior officer and ordered his platoon to cover Pack Leader's escape from a rival drug lord in the area they were operating from. Grinder spent six months in military jail and Pack Leader got out after his last tour. From '68 to the present, they have spent their time building up the Wild Wolves biker gang.

Grinder actually helped Sheriff Manning root out the Wild Goose biker gang up in Story that was producing heroine and LSD in the mountains. Of course, at the time, Sheriff Manning didn't know that Pack Leader wanted to replace them. He just thought Grinder wanted help getting one of his boys off the hook for drunk and disorderly after they were arrested in the city park one night.

When the Gooses were pushed out of Story, what was left of the gang tried to open up shop in Rawlins and were quickly taken out and put in the state penitentiary. That's why when Freeburger threatened to have Grinder and his boys rounded up by the highway patrol and put there, they hightailed it out of Wyoming as fast as they could. The five of them would not have lasted long with over thirty-five Wild Goose members serving time there.

Pack Leader jumps off his chair and walks out to the middle of the camp area to meet Grinder. "So, you think you can take a year off, cost me a couple grand in lawyer fees, and just show up like nothing ever happened?"

Grinder knows the drill just a well as Pack Leader. He stops in front of him, looks him up and down, and says, "You know, I never did like your mouth." Then he hauls back and smashes Pack Leader in the side of the face with a heavy right cross. Pack Leader rolls with the punch and uses the momentum to spin around and crack Grinder in the jaw with an equally powerful back fist. Like two bulls out on the prairie both men collide into one another, punching, kicking, and mauling the other with everything they have. The fight lasts about ten minutes, but in the end Pack Leader is able to clock Grinder so hard that he falls over backward and hits the ground hard.

A couple minutes later, two things are sure. One, Pack leader is still in charge; and two, Grinder is still his second, because nobody else there has ever even come close to lasting that long with Pack Leader. He sees that Grinder is waking up and looks at a couple of the new guys. "You boys show my second-in-command some respect and help him into the cabin over there, then grab us a case of beer. Grinder and I have a lot to talk about."

They start moving before Pack Leader finishes telling them what to do. He smiles and gives himself a "that-a-boy" and he thinks how he just saved Grinder's reputation. God knows he couldn't control all these assholes himself. He'd end up killing half of them, and that would just be bad for business.

Thirty minutes later, Pack Leader and Grinder are in the main cabin of the camp with the doors closed and enjoying some ice-cold beers. He looks at his second and says, "I've seen men clock you across the head with a board, and you'd just smile and then break every bone in their body. How the hell did that deputy dog rookie beat you down the stairs like that? It took me ten minutes, and now that no one is listening, it could have gone either way out there with us. I'm going to be one sore dog in the morning."

Grinder shakes his head, takes a long draw from his can, and puts it down. "I gave you everything I had out there, boss, no holds barred. I'm glad you won, though, because I don't have the head to run all these boys and deal with the assholes across the border. As for that kid, I don't have any excuses. I should have been able to knock him out of his boots, but it was like being attacked by a wild animal. You remember when we were up in Yellowstone a couple of years ago and those stupid tourists were feeding the bears?"

Pack Leader lets out a beer belch. "Yes, and I remember how stupid you were when you rode over there to bitch them out for it and the bear jumped you. It took all of us to ride over there and scare that damn thing off. You were laid up for weeks."

Grinder shakes his head. "It was like the exact same thing. There was no give in that bear. I couldn't stop it. That damn deputy was just like that. He had the same look in his eyes. If Freeburger hadn't pulled him off, I think he'd a killed me with his bare hands."

Pack Leader sits back and remembers and tells Grinder about a wild Vietnamese boy who attacked his battalion with nothing but a machete. They were marching in the bush after raiding a village. Apparently one of his boys got ahold of the mother and showed her a pretty rough time. The kid couldn't have been more than fifteen, but he cut through three of his men to get to the one who hurt his mom. They managed to shoot him several times, but he still made it to his mom's attacker and partially severed his head from his body with one slice. He was going for the head between his legs when Pack Leader himself ended up putting a bullet between the kid's eyes. He still has nightmares about that kid. They found out later that he was one of the few kids in the village who went to school and was in line to study medicine to be a doctor someday. He wasn't a half-crazed dope addict of any kind, just one pissed-off little bastard with blood in his eyes.

"You know, Grinder, we tell each other that we're all like the Vikings that raided England and Europe hundreds of years ago. They had a word for what you're saying. It was 'berserkergang.' It's when those guys would go into battle and some of them would totally lose it. They didn't care if they lived or died. They just wanted at the enemy no matter what. That's what I saw over in Nam. You have to kill those bastards to stop them."

Grinder sits up and gets an excited gleam in his eyes. "Okay, so we go up there in the middle of the night and blow up his cabin while they're all sleeping."

Pack Leader throws his empty beer can at Grinder's head. "Sometimes you're a thickheaded bastard. You do it like that and every gun in Sheridan County will be out for Wolf blood. No, we need a plan that'll keep the cops in check and the people scared. We're there to make money, first and foremost. You being behind bars has slowed our Bighorn operation way down. Our suppliers across the border are getting antsy. I got to go meet with them tomorrow, and you're coming too."

"Oh, for fucks sake, Seth. I can't stand those taco eaters. Do I have to?" Pack Leader glares at him like he's going to start beating on him again and Grinder throws both hands up in the air and says, "Okay, boss. Whatever you say."

One Day Later, Thirty-five Miles South Over the Mexican Border, Altar Municipality Police Station

Renaldo Manerez has come a long way in the last fifteen years since joining up with the Medellin Cartel in Colombia. At the ripe age of fifty-six, he is now a chief lieutenant in charge of the territories of Guatemala, Honduras, Mexico, and the Rocky Mountain region of the United States. All drug smuggling and arms sales in those regions under the Medellin Cartel are under his supervision. Señor Escobar himself sent word that he wanted the Rocky Mountain region of the United States to increase their business by at least 50 percent in the next twelve months. The Wild Wolves biker gang is his key transport and production arm in that territory, and there was a little bit of a hiccup in production last year in the Bighorns with one of their leaders being in jail.

He sits at the police chief's desk in Altar municipality, waiting for Pack Leader and his culprit lieutenant, Grinder, to show up for their meeting. Behind him is his very impatient seventeen-year-old son, Maximillian, and sitting in front of him is a mysterious Russian man who he was told to meet with and give a large sum of cash to. Renaldo and his son, Maximillian, can't help but feel spooked around this man. He is about six feet tall with dark hair and probably in his late twenties. Although his expression is completely unreadable, something in his eyes tells Renaldo that he is a killer of the highest quality. He can only assume that Señor Escobar had hired him for some assassination work and wants his top man in the region to make sure he gets paid.

He reaches under his desk, pulls out a black leather bag with two million in unmarked American bills and hands it to him. The man receives the bag with an almost imperceptible smile and thanks Renaldo.

Renaldo hears the sound of Harley Davidson motorcycles coming up the street. He looks at Maximillian. "Son, please go out and escort Pack Leader and Grinder to this office. Tell the rest to wait outside."

The Russian man stands up. "I do not want to be seen by anyone else, so I will excuse myself. One short question though, if I may?"

Renaldo recognizes this man as someone who his boss values very much and therefore is eager to comply. "By all means. If I can answer I will."

The man looks both men over. "If I understand the operation with the American biker gangs properly, their function is threefold—to transport the drugs and chemicals into the United States, distribute them to the dealers or processors, and then transport the profits back to you. Is that correct?"

Renaldo looks at his son and smiles. "Why yes, that's their function in the Medellin Cartel. Why do you ask?"

The Russian man says, "It just seems to me that a bunch of high-profile bikers doing all that delicate work with their loud, obnoxious motorcycles is a tremendous risk, and so is the fact that you have the same group both transporting product out and money in. Then, trying to hide all that in the chassis of a Harley Davidson chopper must severely limit the amount of product and cash you can move in any one transport."

Renaldo cannot deny that this Russian brings up some good points about the bottlenecking effect of using biker gangs for this kind of work, but he has not been able to come up with a better plan. "Señor, with the way they are training dogs today and some of the newer technology coming out, it is very hard to smuggle these kinds of things in and out of the US. We have been successful of late with the arrangement we have with the biker gangs. They are loud and obnoxious, yes, but they are also feared. Even the police in the western states try to leave them alone if they can."

The Russian turns to leave. "Fear is a powerful ally," he says, "if you employ it properly and with discretion. I wish you good fortune in your endeavors. Please inform Señor Escobar that I will not be available for freelance work for the next couple of years. My country is sending me to the Far East and I do not know when I can return to this region. Goodbye, Señor Manerez." He nods at both of them and quickly leaves out the back before some of the Wild Wolves see him.

"What's that man's name, Father?"

Renaldo lets out a gasp of air. "Señor Escobar called him the Chameleon. That's all I care to know. Now, go do what I told you to do."

Maximillian walks out to the front parking lot of the police station and waves Pack Leader over to him. There are five others who made the trip down with him and Grinder, and their entrance into town did not go unnoticed by the suspicious and weary residents. The police were aware of the biker gangs coming to town, so they were not concerned, but they made an effort to be outside to show the people that they had the situation under control. When Pack Leader and Grinder get to Maximillian, he tells them his father's instructions that the five others wait outside, and he escorts the two of them in.

Grinder never likes being in Mexico. The air is too hot, and the people always look at his blond hair and blue eyes and decide he's the enemy, which by his reckoning he is; but that should not give them the stones to treat him like that. Granted, the last few times he was down here he raised some hell and had his way with a few fine señoritas. Pack Leader told him to rein it in this time. He knows the consequences if he doesn't.

Pack Leader walks right up to the police chief's desk. "Renaldo, we're here. What can the Wild Wolves do for our best supplier?"

Renaldo takes a deep drag from the cigar he is smoking, blows out a couple of smoke circles, and smiles while he ignores him and looks at the other biker. "Grinder, I understand that you let a rookie get the best of you in a fight in front of half the sheriff's department in Sheridan County last week. Would you like to tell me how you can rely on those boys being afraid of you and your gang after that?"

Pack Leader steps forward. "Renaldo, we have the situation under control. This spring...."

Renaldo holds up his hand, stopping him in midsentence, and continues. "Let him answer for himself, please."

Grinder knows he has to control himself right now because this is big money he's talking to, and Pack Leader's patience only goes so far. "Renaldo, that kid is some kind of a lunatic, and he caught me off guard, but I promise you when we get up there next spring, he'll regret ever meeting me."

Renaldo likes what he is hearing, but after getting his orders from Señor Escobar, he knows it will be too little too late to accomplish his goals. He looks at both men and takes another drag from his cigar. "We are going to try a different approach. Sheridan County, Wyoming, and especially Story, is a hotbox now, and we want to keep it that way. Pack Leader, we want you guys to go up there this spring and scare the hell out of those people. You're still going to be transporting drugs in and money out, but not nearly as much as before. We've contracted two other gangs—the Bush Hogs and the Scarecrows—to sneak into Cody and Casper. They'll distribute the goods from those two vantage points while you boys keep all the attention on Sheridan, and especially Story."

In Nam, Pack Leader was as crooked as the hind leg of a dog, but he was also a very intelligent officer. He knows exactly what he is being asked to do and does not like it one bit. "You think for one minute that I'm going to go back up there with all my boys and just lay their heads on the lawman's chopping block so that you can give my contract to a bunch of ass-kissing second stringers? You're crazy, old man."

Despite his father's obvious humor over Pack Leader's outrage, Maximillian cannot stand anyone talking to him like that, so he pulls out his .45 caliber 911 and points it at the biker. "When people talk to my father like that, they die, gringo!"

Renaldo casually reaches up and pushes his son's gun down to his side. "Maximillian, your outrage on my account is appropriate, but I haven't finished yet. Everybody just calm down. Seth, just hear me out. You will always run our operations in the northwestern part of the United States. We just need time to set up a more permanent distribution network. At one time, we thought Sheridan County would be ideal, but since Grinder here got carried away on Sheriff Manning and some civilians, we had to rethink things. There is really no way to quiet down that area now, but we can use that to our advantage. You two go up there and make all the noise you want. Kill some people, rape some girls, and make sure all eyes are on the bikers in Sheridan County. Then when the time is right, we pull you two out. At that point, we will pay you the second part of this installment."

He reaches under the desk and pulls out two bags similar to the one he gave the Russian moments ago. Pack Leader and Grinder open theirs to see several stacks of hundred-dollar bills. "There is one million dollars apiece there. When you're done causing havoc and are safely away, there will be another two million waiting for each of you." He then takes another long drag on his cigar as both men greedily fondle their money. "Pack Leader, whatever is left of your club, plus the additional other two biker gangs, will be totally under your management."

Pack Leader looks over to Grinder, who smiles and nods his head, then turns back to Renaldo. "Okay, Renaldo, you got a deal."

Renaldo smiles and turns and winks at his son then looks back at the two bikers. "Remember, you can't leave the area until we tell you we're ready. You'll have to use your mountain camps to hide out in from time to time, and you'll lose some of your men. But all truly great endeavors in business require some sacrifice. Señor Escobar is going to be watching this venture very closely. But as you can see, he is willing to be very generous for a profitable outcome."

Pack Leader and Grinder leave the office and head back to the five men waiting for them. The bikers look at their two leaders, waiting for anything that will tell them what this is all about. Pack Leader looks over at Grinder, winks, pulls a pack of hundreds out of his bag and throws some bills at each guy. "Are you guys ready to get rich? Because Señor Escobar wants to make us all fat and sassy. What do you say?"

Grinder throws back his head and gives a big howl, and the rest of the Wild Wolves follow his lead. The seven men then get on their choppers and ride away.

Back inside the police station, Maximillian is standing at the window, watching the bikers ride away. He turns his head and says over his shoulder, "Is this really going to work, Father? I am beginning to see why the Russian was questioning our methods. Maybe there's a more efficient way to move our product and money in and out of the United States."

Renaldo takes a big drag off his cigar before smashing the butt into the police chief's tea cup on the desk. "Maximillian, Señor Escobar and I have had countless conversations about this very thing. He is currently looking into a more reliable money-laundering network on the East Coast of the States. As for smuggling our product in, I've been looking at some property around Falcon Lake that borders Texas. My people have discovered some previously unknown subterranean caves that might be ideal for our needs in that category." He holds his index finger to his lips and makes a *shhh* sound. "Señor Escobar is not aware of this, and I want to keep this secret in our family for now."

Maximillian gets a gleam in his eye. "Of course, Father. I would love to see this property and those caves someday. It sounds very exciting."

"Oh, you will, son. And yes, it is very exciting news."

Chapter Four
Family Matters

Jim takes his boots off and tiptoes through the front door of Linda's mother's house to make his way back to his and Linda's room. Thunder gets up from his dog bed and walks over and rubs his head against Jim's thigh. He reaches down and pats his friend on the head and lets him out for a couple minutes to do his business, then brings the dog back in and settles him down again.

He has been on the night shift lately at the sheriff's department, but he also has been spending a lot of time at Sheridan Community College, working on restoring cars and trucks in the auto body department. He and Linda have decided that they want to buy a house someday , and this was a good way to get some extra cash. The used car manager at Sheridan Autos told him that if he wanted to restore some older vehicles the way he did his truck, he would buy them at good market wholesale value. So he worked out the same deal with the college auto body department that he had before, and they are currently on their third project since September of '73.

He already has over eighteen hundred dollars in the bank from the sale of the first two units and expects a much larger pay for his current project, a 1956 Ford Fairlane convertible. Being thrifty, he worked out another deal with the dealership's wash

41

bay to come in on the weekends when he was off and detail the units he restored. He made an extra forty-five dollars apiece for the units he cleaned, and the dealership supplied the equipment and chemicals. Combining the sheriff's deputy pay with his extra moonlighting, Jim and Linda are in a good position to be home-owners very soon. But he's been putting in sixteen combined work hours a day for the last three months.

He notices a light on under the door and is not surprised to see that Linda is still awake at midnight. He opens the door. "You up studying, honey?"

She looks up and smiles as she replies. "No, I finished my accounting homework hours ago. I've been working on our budget, and I wanted to talk to you about some things."

Jim gives a sigh, because he knows that he won't get some sleep until after two, but he tells her he'll hurry up and shower.

When he's finished, he walks back in the room to find Jacob sitting on his side of the bed, eagerly waiting for him. He eyeballs Linda with a disapproving stare, but she just comments that he has not seen his father in two days and heard the shower so here he is. Jim smiles and says, "Okay, Little Chunk, you can sit up with Mommy and me while we talk."

Jacob claps his hands and jumps from the bed into his daddy's arms. They both settle in next to Linda as she shows Jim what she has figured out. She points to some figures on the notebook. "At the rate you're going, we'll have over five thousand in the bank by summer."

Jim gets excited. "So, we'll have our down payment, and we can get a house, right?"

She takes the pencil and puts it to her lips in a thoughtful gesture. "Yes, if we want to go that route. But we have no real credit built up, and that means we'll need a cosigner. Your dad is willing and so is my mom. But they have done so much in

helping us with school, I don't like asking for more. If you can keep this pace up for another three or four more years, we can buy outright. Mom paid only fifteen thousand for this three-bedroom house here in Story. If we want to live in Sheridan, we can get something similar for between twenty and twenty-five thousand. That might take another year. I'll be working full-time when Jacob starts school next year, so you can slow down a little then."

Jim does some quick calculations in his head. "It seems to me that we'll have what we need in two and a half years, not three."

Linda smiles at her husband's quick calculating mind but adds, "Yes, if we don't pay taxes on your extra income; but you know how I feel about that."

"But Linda, the guys at Sheridan Autos told me people do work for them all the time under the table and no one ever gets in trouble."

She then reminds him that the wife-beater, Bob Jones, who he helped arrest last year, was caught doing engine work for people around Sheridan and never reported a dime of his income. He ended up having to sell his mobile home to cover his IRS fines. Now he's living in the Crescent Hotel and is barely able to keep up with alimony and child support since his wife divorced him.

"Okay, okay, we'll make sure Uncle Sam, Mother Wyoming, and Sister Sheridan County all get their cut. Better safe than sorry. But I won't stop giving my tithe to Pastor Jim's church. He's been there since before I was born, and I can actually understand what he is talking about in his sermons."

Linda laughs and puts an affectionate hand on her husband's cheek. "I would never ask you to stop giving to the church, Jim." She points to the sheet she is working on. "See, I already accounted for all of our tithing from both our incomes now and in the future."

Jim lays Little Chunk down because he has fallen asleep in his arms while his mommy and daddy were talking. Adoringly, he stares at his wife. "When you get that associate degree in accounting next year, I hope you don't go to work for the government. You'll shock the whole damn country by balancing the budget and pissing every politician off from here to Washington."

With that said, they tuck in Little Chunk, give each other a goodnight kiss, and go to sleep.

The next day, Jim is enjoying one of his few days off with his family. Linda decides to cook Jim's favorite meal for lunch—fried chicken, mashed potatoes with gravy, green beans, oven rolls, and apple pie. Jim, Little Chunk, and Thunder are out in the backyard doing some chores and Jim is beginning to lose his mind over the myriad of smells coming from the kitchen.

After the lawn is mowed and raked, the two boys and their dog find themselves in the garage, putting stuff away. Jacob finds a box of his dad's old boxing equipment and pulls out a set of smaller gloves that almost fit his hands. He gets them halfway on and comes over and starts pounding on his dad's leg. At first Jim thinks that it's kind of cute, but then Jacob hauls back and pops him in the thigh and almost takes his leg out from underneath him. Thunder is yelping and licking Jacob like he wants him to keep it up.

Jim reaches down and rubs his leg a little. "You have a heck of a right there, Little Chunk." He looks around to make sure Linda isn't anywhere near, then bends down and says, "You want your old man to show you how to do that the right way?"

Jacob vigorously nods his head and Jim quietly gets some of the boxing equipment out and takes him and Thunder to the backyard.

Five minutes later, they are behind some bushes over by the fence where Linda can't see what's going on from the house. Jim is down on his knees, holding a couple of boxing trainer focus pads in front of Jacob. Jacob is doing everything he can to knock his dad's hands into the next century.

"That's right. Put your right foot back and keep it shoulder width from the other foot. Point your back toes at your target and stay on the ball of your foot. Now put your left foot forward and curve it slightly inward. Every time you throw a punch, push forward with your rear leg, but keep both knees bent."

Jacob does what his dad says. He shoots both elbows out sideways, hauls back, and pushes two strong punches into the pads. Jim feels the difference from the correct leg positioning and now starts to work on the proper punch technique.

"Okay, now put both hands up here by your eyebrows and extend your left hand about a foot in front of the right." He places his pad on Jacob's left hand first and says, "This is your speed." Then he does the same on the right hand and says, "This is your power. When you throw a punch, keep your elbows in and use your whole body to launch the fist into the target."

Jacob stares at his dad like he is speaking Greek. Jim takes off the focus pads and grabs his son's hands and pulls them forward from the position he just showed him. He takes the fists and makes them turn horizontal as he pulls them forward. Then he tells Jacob to lean into the punches as they are thrown instead of hauling back and throwing.

Jacob is smart as a whip and catches on quickly. Jim finally thinks he's got the right idea, so he lets go of his son's hands; but before he can reach down and get the focus pads on, Jacob squares up and with almost perfect form throws a left jab, followed immediately by a right cross into the side of his daddy's chin. With all his body levers in sync, Jim gets the full impact of all Jacob's forty-two pounds into his face. Not expecting the impact, he has no chance to roll with the punch. He falls over sideways to the grassy ground. Thunder immediately starts yelping and dancing like they are both playing with him.

Of course, Jacob thinks his daddy is playing and jumps on him and starts to pummel him with more punches. Jim is so excited about what his son just did that he ignores his sore jaw and bends Jacob to the ground and starts to mercilessly tickle him. Of course Thunder joins in and starts howling at full volume.

A rather loud clearing of the throat is heard over the commotion. Both boys and the dog look up to see a very unhappy Linda standing over them with a rolling pin covered in whole wheat flour. With all the boxing paraphernalia scattered around, Jim has no recourse. He just looks at his wife and says, "I'm sorry, honey. We were done with chores and just horsing around."

She takes the rolling pin and shakes it at him. "Horsing around, huh? And then you teach our four-year-old how to knock a grown man off his knees? What if he does that to Grandpa or a teacher or something, you big lug-head?"

Jacob gets up, takes the gloves off, and runs over to his mommy. He grabs her hand and looks back at his dad. "Daddy, you can't hide anything from mommy."

At that, the couple stare at one another for a few more seconds and then burst out in laughter.

When Linda gets hold of herself, she tells Jim there are a couple of highway patrolmen on motorcycles out front to meet him. "That'd be the new motorcycle unit Al told me about," he says. He gets up and walks around to the front of the house.

Linda looks down at her little boy and gives him a sad smile. "Well, I knew your daddy was going to teach you that stuff someday. Just didn't expect it so soon." She then gets a wicked gleam in her eye, reaches down, picks him up, and balances him on her left hip as she turns to walk into the house. "So, you can knock Daddy on his butt now. Can't tell ya how many times I wanted to do that."

Jim walks out front and sees two Wyoming highway patrolmen sitting on brand-spanking new Yamaha 350 Enduro motorcycles. One of them gets off his bike, takes his helmet off and walks up to Jim with his hand extended. "Jim Edwards, I don't know if you remember me, but I graduated two years before you did. Joe Mason."

Jim grabs the big guy's hand. "How in the hell could anyone forget the only quarterback in twenty years who led the Sheridan Broncs to the state championship?"

They both laugh, and Joe says, "Yes, but we did lose that game, if you remember, 20 to 14."

Jim immediately shoots back. "Yes, but we did stop Natrona from getting that extra point in the last five seconds."

Joe gets a half smile on his face. "Well, we did do that, didn't we? Let me introduce you to my partner, Jerry Gibes, from Casper."

Jim looks at both men and then his jaw drops. "Wait a minute! Jerry Gibes was the name of the quarterback for the Natrona County Mustangs. Are you kidding me? They made you two partners? Someone's got a sick sense of humor."

The other patrolman gets off his bike and takes off his helmet. "That's what I said. But you know, old Joe here kind of grows on you after a while. There's only one thing I like better than football, and that's riding motorcycles. So, when this detail came up, my hand shot up and so did Joe's. I guess we're destined to be together, one way or another."

For the next half hour, the three men discuss the logistics of Story and the biker gang problem that plagues the area. Sheridan still has not put in a repeater radio signal booster for the sheriff's department in Story, but the highway patrol has a much larger budget and installed theirs that winter. They lent Jim one of their TI Motorola handheld radios, which allows him to stay in contact with their dispatch and all the patrolmen, including Joe and Jerry.

Jim walks over to his squad car, gets an envelope out of his file box, and walks back over to the highway patrolmen. "These are the two varmints we're on the lookout for." He shows them pictures of Pack Leader and Grinder, taken a couple of years ago. "They are the number one and number two men of the Wild Wolves biker gang that came in here after we booted the Wild Gooses out."

Jerry grabs the picture of Pack Leader. "Isn't this the one that helped Sheriff Manning catch those Goose boys cooking meth back up in the canyon?"

Jim says, "Yes, but he just assumed that Pack Leader was trading info to get one of his boys released from a drunk-and-disorderly charge back then."

All three lawmen know that deals like that go on all the time, and no one would ever blame Manning for that. As they are discussing patrol routes, a Sheridan County sheriff's car pulls up, and Al Freeburger steps out. "Afternoon, boys."

Al leans back against the hood of his squad car, takes off his hat, and rubs his hand across the top of his crew-cut hair. "Boys, we have a big problem. State Representative Martin Reno just filed charges against Manning for corruption and dereliction of duty in the case where he released the Wild Wolves boy two years ago. With all the trouble we had last year with that gang, he's saying that Manning was paid off, and is accusing him of being in business with them in their dope dealing."

Jim pushes away from his own squad car. "Lieutenant, that's pure bullshit. Everybody knows that the sheriff did that so he could get the location of the Gooses' dope kitchen. Nobody knew that Pack Leader was going to move in and take over."

Al says, "Well, I wouldn't give a plugged nickel for that slimy carpetbagger, Reno. He moved up here from Arizona eight years ago and started sticking his nose into everything. He tried to run for mayor once but failed, and then former governor Arson appointed him as a rep just before the gubernatorial election and right after State Rep Tom Reatle died. Hell, I don't think he could win a fair election in this county if he tried. That's probably why he's trying to defame Manning."

Jim leans back against his squad car, puts his hand to his chin and looks over at Al quizzically. "I don't know, Lieutenant. Sheriff Manning is an institution around here. If Reno fails, he's done for good. There's got to be more to it than that."

"Nobody ever accused you of being stupid, kid. That's why I want you with me when we go down to Cheyenne for Manning to testify before the State Board of Inquiry. Something is rotten in the state capital, and I think that some pencil-pushing politicians are taking scraps from a pack of Wolves lately. We need to figure out who, and then take them down."

While Al is talking, Linda comes running out of the house, frantic with tears running down her face. She races over to Jim and tells him that someone from Coffeen School just called, and her mother had a heart attack and is being flown to Billings, Montana, for treatment.

Al walks over to the couple. "You two get your boy and get out of here. Me and the highway patrol will handle things until you get back."

Jim thanks Al profusely. "What about that board of inquiry?"

Al tells him that it's next month and he'll figure it out with him later.

Billings, Montana, General Hospital ICU Unit

They leave Jacob with Jim's parents and race up to Billings as fast as they can. Sadly, Linda's mom could not hold on until they got there. When they run into the hospital, an older Asian man whom they both recognize as Martha's cardiologist, Dr. Roho, is waiting for them in the lobby. After he explains that she had already passed, Linda stands there for a few moments in shock, not knowing what to say or do. Jim gently takes her hand as Dr. Roho motions them to the room where her mother's body is still lying on the bed.

They both stand there stiff as boards for what seems like an eternity with completely unreadable expressions. Linda turns to look at her husband and sees that tears are now starting to roll down his face. She buries her head in his shoulder and finally allows herself to cry. They knew that Martha had been dealing with heart disease for a while now. At first, they thought that living with her might be too much, but she would not hear any of that and insisted that they stay, which they did. Linda looks into her husband's eyes and says that at least she got to enjoy her only grandchild for four and a half years. Jim takes his big arms and pulls her closer, kisses the top of her head, and says, "He'll never forget her, either."

The memorial service for Martha Pasquali was held at the Holy Name Catholic Church in Sheridan, Wyoming, on March 21, 1974. Her family buried her in the Kendrick Cemetery that afternoon. Several days later, while going over her will and financial records, they found out two rather astonishing details. She had taken all the money that they paid her in rent for the last five years and put it into a trust fund for their family. At two hundred dollars a month, the total with interest was $13,500. She also left everything she had to the couple, which included her house in Story and some property and assets back East.

Linda found out that her mother only had about three thousand left to pay on the house, so she and Jim paid off the mortgage. It took a long time to help little Jacob understand that his grandmother was gone and was not coming back. Several times over the next few weeks they would go to his room and hold him as he cried himself back to sleep.

On May 4 that spring, Jim and Al went with Sheriff Manning to testify at the Wyoming State Board of Inquiry. Linda took Jacob and flew back East to settle her mother's affairs there.

Chapter Five
Ghost Bikers

Bighorn Mountain Range, Montana, May 1974

Pack Leader and Grinder are getting their backpacks and gear set for their 125-mile hike from Fort Smith, Montana, to Story, Wyoming, down the Bighorn Mountain range. They just met up with the group that smuggles some of the Medellin Cartel drugs and money up and down the Continental Divide from Canada to Mexico, about a hundred miles west of their current position.

Pack Leader put Grinder in charge of picking who would make this trip with them. He had to think about that one. Going cross-country on a Harley can be physically taxing, but it's nothing compared to hiking 125 miles through a mountain range with a hundred-pound backpack. Most of his boys in the Wild Wolves had big, muscular arms and could hit like a mule but hadn't done any kind of hiking since they were in the service. The boys he picked had all been discharged from the army or marines within the last year, and he was confident they could all handle this hike.

The biggest thing bugging the group is that they have just spent the last three days in old cargo vans. Renaldo had them meet up with his people at the Divide so that they can get some of the drugs they are going to be carrying and take them to the Story distribution center. The plan is to hike into their deepest camp west of Story and begin their operation from there. Some of the other members of the club have already smuggled their choppers into the little mountain town. The mystique of them showing up on their bikes without anyone knowing how they got there is their proposed method of scaring the hell out of everyone. Pack Leader knows that Manning and Freeburger have every law enforcement agency in Wyoming looking for him and Grinder to show up in Sheridan County. And show up he will, but they won't know how or when.

Grinder grabs his gear, puts it against a tree, and looks over at Pack Leader. "That was a lot of dough you gave that candy-ass state rep and his buddy in the AG's office. Renaldo usually reimburses us for bribes to politicians, but since he doesn't know about this one, it's all on us."

Pack Leader motions Grinder to the other side of the van where the five other guys with them can't hear what they are saying. "Listen, one thing is certain. Our boys don't die for anyone but us. Those greasy wetbacks down south can kiss my ass if they're thinking that any of the Wild Wolves are going to be sacrificed for them. Besides, you think you and I could control those other biker gangs he said we get by ourselves?"

Grinder is looking at his boots, listening intently. "Hell no. If it's just you and me left, they'll kill us and then their leaders will tell Renaldo we died fighting the cops or something."

Pack Leader pats him on the back. "This way Manning and Freeburger will be down in Cheyenne for a couple of weeks, and we'll start off by killing the Boy Scout in Story, along with his wife and kid. Then we do exactly what Renaldo told us to and get everyone's attention on us. But before the local cops can do any serious damage, we'll get the hell out of Dodge, collect our two million each, and still have most of our boys with us. Hell, if we play our cards right, with the extra two gangs in our pack, we'll rival the Hells Angels as far as being the biggest club in the country." They both take each other's forearms and give the old warrior handshake and then return to unloading their gear.

The seven bikers, now turned cross-country hikers, set out on their 125-mile trek. Grinder looks at all the men. "Nobody ever accused us bikers of being the most hygienic people in the world, but we're all old soldiers. I brought plenty of soap, so we're not showing up in Story smelling like those assholes over on the Divide. I swear those guys go for months without taking a bath. I'll bet the bears get the hell out of their way." He hefts his pack on, and looks over at Pack Leader who nods, smiles, throws his head back, and gives a wolf howl. Everyone joins in. "Okay, ladies, let's go!"

The hike took two and a half weeks.

May 18, 1974, Story, Wyoming

Seven much leaner Wild Wolves descend from the last of the Bighorn Mountain trails into the little town of Story just north-west of the fish hatchery. Pack Leader and Grinder tell the others to hunker down and set up a staging camp as they stow their gear and change into some western casual clothes, shave their beards, and cut their hair. With their cowboy boots, ball caps, long-sleeve denim shirts and Levi's jeans, all their tattoos are covered up nicely. When the duo walks into town that morning, no one will ever recognize either one. Neither has been without facial hair since getting out of the military almost seven years ago. To the locals, they look like the myriad of out-of-towners who start showing up this time of year for fishing, camping, or rodeoing in the local area.

They start out on Penrose Lane and walk onto Fish Hatchery Road, which is where their contacts say they rented a barn that all their equipment, weapons, personal belongings, and most importantly, their bikes are stowed. Pack Leader walks up to the property, opens the mailbox, and pulls out a large, tan envelope. Inside he finds keys and a Wild Wolves jacket patch in it. "This is it. All our stuff is inside."

Grinder throws his head back and gives the wolf howl, grabs the keys out of Pack Leader's hand, and runs to the door. When he gets inside, he runs through the barn and past all the stuff right to the bikes, locates his own bike, hops on and starts to kick-start it.

Pack Leader walks up and grabs the key from the ignition. "What the fuck do you think you're doing, dumb-ass?" Grinder almost takes a swing at him, but the biker boss holds both hands up. "We can't be seen in the open on these yet. Nobody can know that this is where we are hiding them. Remember, we're the 'ghost biker gang' that no one saw come into town!"

Grinder sits back in his seat and looks down at the gas tank between his legs and shakes his head. "I'm sorry, boss. I just haven't seen her in a while and I got the itch, you know what I mean?"

Pack Leader walks over to his own bike and affectionately runs his hand across the dark brown hand-molded leather seat and then over the custom-painted gas tank. "No problem, Todd. Don't worry, we're all going out tonight and the Boy Scout and his family are the ones who are going to be pushing up daisies."

Over in the corner of the barn are a couple of 1968 VW Vanagons with Florida plates on them. Grinder looks over at them and then back at his boss and throws both hands in the air as he exclaims, "You got to be fucking kidding me! What if we get into a chase or something? Those damn things can barely do sixty-five on the flats."

Pack Leader gets a big grin on his face, walks over, and pops the hood on the closest one as he motions Grinder over. When he gets close enough, he sees that the little four-cylinder German engine has been replaced by a Chevy small-block 283 eight-cylinder. After further inspection, he sees that the engine has a Holley 750 quad pumper carburetor, and there's a dual exhaust hidden under the vehicle. Pack Leader says, "They also have a high performance, four-speed transmission and clutch. These babies will get up and go if we need them to, but they still look like the old lady jalopies we need them to be. Compliments of our friend's money down south."

In the early evening, two vans pull up to the trail leading to the staging camp that Pack Leader and Grinder left that morning. There to greet them are five very different looking men to the ones they left. Each man is clean-shaven and sporting a military-style crew cut. They all have on cowboy boots, long sleeve denim shirts, and Levi's. They all also have ball caps on. They begin to stow their gear in one van. One of the men rides with Grinder and the gear, and the other four get in with Pack Leader.

They go to the barn first, unload all their gear, and park one of the vans inside. Then they head over to the Wagon Box Inn on Highway 340 to get something to eat and also to get some intel on Jim Edwards and his family. They are all pretty excited to be at a bar and grille, because none of them have had a steak or a beer in over three weeks. Grinder tells all the guys that they are undercover right now and not to go in acting like a bunch of rowdy bikers. "You see why I made all you assholes wash up every day on the trail? These people know what a stink bomb a deep forest hiker is when he comes off the trail, and we want them all to think we're just a bunch of boys from back East visiting the Wild West."

They enter the tavern nice and gentle like and find a big table at the far end of the dining room next to the jukebox. Much to all their displeasure, someone has about umpteen songs stacked up on the machine's 45 rpm turntable and they are all by The Carpenters. When they sit down, "Top of the World" starts to play, and everyone has to fight the temptation to kick the jukebox and ruin the record.

When the waitress comes over to the table, they see that she is a gorgeous blonde with a full figure and is definitely excited to have a table full of clean-cut, handsome men to wait on. She asks them what they are all drinking and simultaneously they all say "BEER!"

Pack Leader leans forward and says, "Honey, just give us a couple of pitchers of your best stuff on tap and keep it coming. Oh, seven steaks too, medium rare!"

She winks at him and heads back to the bar. One of the boys throws back his head to let out a wolf howl but is elbowed by Grinder. "What the fuck did you do that for, Grinder?"

As Pack Leader puts his hand on the guy's mouth, Grinder says, "First names, dipshit. I'm Todd and he's Seth." The biker's eyes get as big as saucers and he vigorously nods.

"Is everything okay here, gentlemen?"

All seven look up to see two Wyoming highway patrolmen standing beside the table. Pack Leader stands up and offers his hand and says, "I'm sorry, officer. My buddy here has had a few and he was going to say something inappropriate to our waitress, so I stopped him."

Before Officer Mason can respond, the waitress returns with some big plates of sizzling steaks in her hands. "It's okay, Joe. These guys are tame compared to a lot of the locals we get in here." Then she looks right at Pack Leader and says, "And a lot cuter."

Joe laughs at Marcy's famous flirtatious nature and says, "Okay, but you know what time of year it is, Marcy. With Jim out of town, we're spread a little thin."

Grinder and Pack Leader both catch the statement and eyeball each other warily. Officer Gibes then steps forward and looks at Pack Leader. "Excuse me, sir, I didn't get your name."

Pack Leader immediately steps forward and offers his hand. "Seth Brown, and this is Todd Wilkinson. Todd, me, and these guys here are college buddies from Florida State. We're here to do some fishing and hiking."

Joe smiles at his partner and then asks them all for some ID. All seven men produce Florida driver's licenses and hand them to the highway patrolmen. Joe looks at each ID very carefully and then passes them back to the men. "Sorry, guys. We're just on the lookout for some pretty nasty bikers who might come around here this spring or summer. But you fellas don't fit their profile at all."

Grinder laughs and pats Gibes on the back. "Well, we sure don't want to run into any of those guys. With all that going on, are you sure just three highway patrolmen are enough to cover this area?"

Joe has to think about that for a minute, and then he remembers Jim. "You must be thinking about when I said we are short-handed because Jim Edwards is out of town right now. He's the sheriff's deputy assigned to this area. His mother-in-law just passed a few weeks back, so his wife and son went back East to settle some affairs; but Jim had to go to Cheyenne with Sheriff Manning and Lieutenant Freeburger. The sheriff is testifying at a board of inquiry. Probably be there for another week or so."

Both the bikers sit back down and do everything in their power to hide the disappointment of not being able to kill the Boy Scout tonight. Joe points outside. "If that's your VW van out there, I hope you don't think that those heavy mud and snow tires are going to make it okay to drive the back-mountain roads. Those things hardly have enough horse power to get up

Dayton-Kane Road northwest of Sheridan. You take that up any of these old logging trails and we'll be coming up to get you out."

Pack Leader stares quizzically at the two officers. "How are you guys going to come get us in your squad cars? They have more horsepower, but they're so low they'll get stuck too."

Officer Gibes motions the group to look outside through the window at the two Yamaha 350 Enduro highway patrol bikes in the parking lot. "Those babies will go anywhere a horse will, only a lot faster."

Joe then says, "We're part of the new Bike Task Force here in Wyoming."

After telling the would-be tourists about their bikes, the two highway patrol officers leave the group alone. Grinder is staring at his steak and playing with it with his fork. "You know, those guys can chase us anywhere we go now. They might just find one of our kitchen camps back up in the mountains."

Pack Leader leans back. "We're here to raise some hell, nothing more. All the real sensitive operations have already been moved to the other two areas." He looks over at the sexy waitress named Marcy, then back at his gang and says, "What do you say we go get into our duds and find a couple more like her and let everybody know the Wolves are back?"

Just before one of the guys is ready to throw his head back and give a wolf cry, Grinder reaches over and places an iron-clamp grip on the man's forearm and fixes him with his best "don't make me kill you" stare.

Later that Night in Piney Creek Canyon, North of Story

Marcy, Brenda, and Wilma are freshmen at the University of Wyoming. Marcy loves partying like all the other girls, but since her parents don't have money like her two friends did, she had to work her whole summer break just to make enough to pay off the remainder of her dorm and meal plan at the university. But tonight is special because it's a girls-only party night—or so they thought.

After leaving the Wagon Box around 10:00 p.m., she meets her friends at the Story post office. They all pile into Marcy's Jeep and head right out to meet some friends from Sheridan who got them some Boone's Farm Strawberry Hill wine. They pay for it and head to their favorite party spot in the canyon up behind Story. What they don't know is that this night will change their lives forever.

Pack Leader is looking through his binoculars at the scene just down the road in Piney Creek Canyon. Three beautiful girls getting drunk all by themselves is enough to excite any biker, and especially one who has been commissioned to cause some chaos and make some noise. He has three of his crew with him on their choppers while Grinder and the other two are headed for Sheridan to make some noise there.

Thanks to the Hollywood makeup kit they had at the barn, all the guys are looking like their normal selves with long hair and beards. He reaches down and gives his fake beard a tug, amazed at how well the skin glue bonds the fake hair to his face and scalp. But it makes sense. The people he bought the kit from were stuntmen makeup artists, and all that stuff has to stay on under extreme circumstances.

All at once, they kick-start their Harley Davidson choppers and begin to rev their engines. "Remember, one of them has to survive so she can tell everybody what happened," Pack Leader says as he and his boys roll into the girl's party site. They leave Marcy alive because she was the one who said Seth was cute at the Wagon Box earlier that evening. Alive means she was still breathing and could talk, but not much more.

Same Evening, Kendrick Cemetery, Sheridan, Wyoming

Grinder doesn't like the fact that Pack Leader chose to stay in Story and sent him and the other two bikers to Sheridan. They are pushing their Harleys to the entrance of the graveyard up behind Big Horn Avenue. It's a Saturday night and there are always some teenagers up there partying. He harassed a group there a couple of years ago and knows he can get out of there before the Sheridan PD or the sheriff's department can respond. They finally see what they are looking for—a flashlight pointed at the ground over by some rich person's grave monument. The soft red glow of a marijuana joint is raised and brightens as one teenager puts it to her mouth and takes a long drag. Like his boss, Grinder is looking like his old self with his long, shaggy, blond hair and bushy beard on. He's also sporting his cut-off Levi's jacket and jeans, exposing his muscular chest and arms.

As the bikers get closer, they see another teen join the group, which makes for four teenagers there—three boys and one girl. They appear to be between sixteen and eighteen years old. As the three are about to start their bikes up, they hear an argument erupting between two of the boys over the girl smoking marijuana.

When Grinder takes a closer look, he sees the problem. Two of the boys have long hair and are wearing wide bell-bottom jeans, brightly colored t-shirts, dark jackets, and headbands. The other boy is in straight-leg jeans, cowboy boots, a white T-shirt, and a tan cowboy hat. The boy in the cowboy hat grabs the girl by the arm and yells at the other two boys while shaking his fist at them. Grinder tells the other two to wait there and he walks over to see what all the fuss is about.

"Put that damn thing down and stomp it out or I will cave your greaser face in, Rodney."

"Tim, get out of my business. Rodney and Albert are my friends and we're not hurting anyone."

"Bullshit, Megan. If Dad found out you were out here smoking weed with these two greasers instead of feeding your horses like he told you to, he'd shoot them and whip you within an inch of your life."

"Tell you what. Give me the girl and the weed. I'll beat the shit out of her two friends, she and I will go party a little, and you can go home and feed her horses."

All four teenagers freeze as a stone-cold chill goes up their spines. They turn and see a large, blond biker sporting his Wild Wolves emblem on his cut-off jean jacket. Rodney drops the joint and then he and Albert take off into the cemetery. Grinder sticks his index finger and thumb into his mouth and blows out an eardrum-splitting whistle, then he turns and motions the other two bikers in the boys' direction. They kick-start their Harleys and take off after them. Grinder walks up to the cowboy kid who, to his amazement, looks more mad than scared.

The cowboy named Tim steps in front of his sister, takes his hat off, and hands it back to her. He looks Grinder in the eye and says, "You ain't getting anywhere near my sister, you biker faggot."

Grinder puts both hands up in a calming gesture and begins to say, "Look, kid, you're going to give me whatever...." Smack! The cowboy hauls off and belts him across the chin with one hell of a good right cross, followed by a left hook and then a right uppercut that knocks him right on his ass. Bewildered, Grinder takes his hand and rubs his chin, then looks up and makes sure he isn't dealing with that crazy deputy again. He looks at him and sees that they do resemble one another, but this kid can't be a day over eighteen.

Tim takes a step toward the biker whom he just knocked on his ass, puts himself in a good fighting stance, and readies himself for the biker to get up again. "You're that asshole Grinder, who my cousin Jim kicked the shit out of a while back. His mom is my mom's sister. Jim is the one who taught me how to box. We were on the same team for years."

One thing that Grinder can always count on with these dumb cowboys is that they like to fight fair. Grinder had no such limiting morals. While the cowboy is waiting for him to get up and finish the fight, he balances himself on both hands and sends a boot right into the boy's crotch. Tim doubles over and grabs his groin as he starts to vomit. Grinder hops up on his feet and starts to move in for the kill. Approaching the boy and ready to deal out death, something smashes into the back of his head and he sees lighting go off and falls face forward. Behind him is Tim's sister with a big tree limb in her hand that she just used on the back of Grinder's head.

She runs over to her brother and helps him up as he is trying to recover from the kick. Grinder gets up on his hands and knees and rubs the back of his head, then brings his hand in front of his face and sees blood. There is a saying in the Wild Wolves, and it goes, "When Grinder sees his own blood, he's going to want to replace it with yours." He jumps up, and like a wild boar, explodes into the two kids.

First, he takes the girl and backhands her so hard across the jaw that she just falls limp to the ground, and then he turns to her brother. "Your dickhead cousin caught me off guard, just like you and your sister did. I couldn't do anything to him because there were too many guns around. But there are no guns around here, so you two are mine."

Tim manages to get up and put up a damn good fight. It takes Grinder five solid minutes to finally knock him out. By the time Grinder is done with him, Tim's face is so swollen you cannot see his eyes and all his top front teeth are gone. Then with blood all over his hands and his fake beard barely attached to his face, Grinder walks over to the half-conscious girl by the gravestone. "Now you and me are going to have ourselves a little party of our own." He proceeds to rip all her clothes off and rapes her right there.

Tim and his sister do survive the attack. They both are taken to Billings, Montana, to undergo medical treatment and prepare for reconstructive surgery to their faces. As for the two other boys, Grinder's men tell him it's good that they caught up to them in the graveyard because that's where they shut their eyes for the last time.

Grinder and his two men meet Pack Leader up at the camp behind the fish hatchery in Story. They have a camouflaged area back there where he decided to keep their biker paraphernalia, including their choppers, hidden. He knows the heat is going to get turned up real fast after tonight. They stow all their gear and proceed to change back into their tourist personas. Grinder, however, has to put on some Hollywood makeup around his chin and eyes to hide the bruises that the cowboy kid gave him earlier. Pack Leader pats him on the back. "As long as you're the one walking away while the other is down, buddy, that's all that counts."

The next day, the front page of the *Sheridan Tribune* reads, "Attacks in Story and Sheridan. Ghost Bikers Molest and Kill. No One Knows How They Got Here."

Chapter Six
Wyoming's Own Dick Tracy

Cheyenne, Wyoming, One Week Earlier

Sheriff Manning tells Al and Jim to wait in the lobby of the state capitol building while he goes to prepare to testify before the State Board of Inquiry. It will be a closed session, so they are not allowed in.

Jim decides to take a look around. He goes out to the parking lot and walks over to the section reserved for the attorney general and his staff. In the AG's spot is a two-year-old Cadillac Eldorado that catches his attention. He heard that John Stalker's family was into oil down in the southwest part of the state and figured he'd be driving something like that, but next to it, in a spot marked Assistant Attorney General Ben Sisko, is something that makes Jim's heart go into his throat. Like a pearl on a velvet pillow covered in sleek Chevy white, sporting mag wheels with some of the blue still on the white lettering, and proprietary racing stripes, is a 1974 Pontiac Firebird two-door hardtop coupe. Upon closer inspection he sees that it has the top-of-the-line, eight-cylinder, 170-horsepower engine. Sheridan Autos had only a couple of the six-cylinder, 100-horsepower models on their lot, so he has been itching to get a look at this model.

Mesmerized by the sleek machine before him, Jim does not notice the man standing next to him until he speaks. "Pretty nice machine, huh? Just picked her up last week. Been wanting one of these since GM came out with the model three years ago."

Jim turns to see a short, stocky man with glasses in his late thirties or early forties. He is also wearing a state government ID that identifies him as Assistant Attorney General Ben Sisko. Jim smiles. "I'm sorry, Mr. Sisko. I just really love nice cars. I do a little restoration on the side, and I saw your boss's Eldorado here and then your Firebird. I wish I had a camera, because my wife would love to see these two beauties sitting next to each other."

"Have we met, Deputy? You're from Sheridan, right?"

"I doubt it, sir. I just came up here with my boss for some kind of an investigation hearing he had to be at. They told my lieutenant and me to wait in the lobby, so I just came out to gawk at the cars."

"Funny you mention that, because I'm headed to the AG's office about that matter with Sheriff Manning, and I'm almost late."

Jim can see the nervousness in the man and decides to press. "Well, please don't let me keep you, but could you tell me how much this puppy set you back? Because in Sheridan they're being advertised for $5,100."

This causes a very self-satisfied grin to manifest itself on Sisko's face. "Well, here they are going for $4,500 each, but a friend of mine and I went in together and got them for $4,000 apiece, even. They only had two of these in stock. I got the white and he got the black. I have to go, Deputy. Nice talking to you. Sorry to hear about the trouble your boss is in. Maybe the AG can figure something out for him. Goodbye."

As Sisko runs up the stairs to the meeting, Jim takes out a notepad, writes down the license plate number on the Firebird and starts walking around the lot to find its dark twin. He finds it in the part of lot designated for state senators and representatives.

The sheriff meets privately with the State Attorney General John Stalker, Assistant AG Ben Sisko, and State Representative Martin Reno in the AG's office before the hearings. There, he is informed that Representative Reno and Assistant Attorney General Ben Sisko felt it necessary to bring him in and question him about making deals with the leader of a notorious biker gang. He explains to the attorney general that Pack Leader traded intel about the Wild Gooses' meth kitchen in Story for the release of one of his gang members who was in jail for drunk and disorderly. The information led to the arrest and conviction of thirty-plus bikers and the closing down of a major northwestern drug distribution ring.

John first looks at his subordinate, Ben Sisko, then at Representative Reno and says, "Boys, you both know that deals like this go on all the time. Sheriff Manning accomplished something up there that is worth the governor's compliments and gratitude, not a State Board of Inquiry. Ben, what the hell were you thinking?"

Before the assistant AG can answer, Representative Reno stands up and says, "Attorney General Stalker, the board of inquiry is not your call in the first place. I agreed to meet with you and your assistant out of courtesy. There are those in the House and Senate who believe that making deals with criminals, no matter what the outcome, is wrong. An example must be set, and I intend to pursue the sheriff's removal from office with the full backing of the Wyoming legislative body's authority."

The AG just huffs at the representative and then stares at his assistant. "Ben, I know you want my job someday, and I'm old enough to say more power to you. But are you really throwing in with this Johnny-come-lately carpetbagging appointee?"

After giving his original statement, George Manning just sat there and did not say a word—mostly because the AG asked him to keep quiet while he questioned the other two. But after his old friend John said that, he has to add, "You know, John, there's no way in hell this asshole will ever win an election in Sheridan County after this. He's got something else up his sleeve. You can bet your bottom dollar on that."

Representative Reno's face turns red. He stands and heads for the door. "You're both going to regret ever knowing me," he says, slamming the door behind as he leaves.

The AG just sighs and says under his breath, "We already do, buddy." He then turns his attention back to his assistant. "Well, what's up, Ben? Are you really so naïve as to climb in bed with that idiot?"

The assistant AG stands up and fidgets with his sport jacket, straightens his glasses, and says in a scared and broken tone, "Law enforcement officers should not break the law to enforce it. That's where I stand, sir." He abruptly turns and almost trips over Manning's chair as he leaves the office.

Now that the two old friends are left in the room, both men can't help but burst out laughing. When Manning finally settles down, he looks over at John. "So, what now?"

"Well, now you go in there and tell the truth and make those boys look like the idiots they are."

The old detective wheels start turning in Manning's head as he looks at his friend. "There is something else going on here, John. Why would those two ruin their careers like this? Seems to me like someone with some deep pockets has paid them off pretty good. We need to find out who and why."

Much to everyone's displeasure, the board of inquiry lasts for almost eight hours. Representative Reno grills Sheriff Manning with a constant badgering of insignificant questions on the details as to how he performs his duties. At the ripe hour of 5:00 p.m., he starts to ask why the sheriff got a divorce from his second wife three years ago. The chairman of the board of inquiry, a twenty-year veteran lawmaker from Johnson County, finally shuts Reno down by adjourning the inquiry until the next day. Even though he was cut off by his superior in a not so professional or legal way, Manning cannot help but notice that Reno seemed very pleased with the outcome. It's almost like he was trying to get the hearings extended another day.

In the morning session the next day, Reno lays out his grievances and accusations against Manning and his department. A few other representatives question him and then Manning is finally allowed to give a statement. It looks like the inquiry is wrapping up and that he will be exonerated, but then Reno brings in the assistant AG to testify, and that extends it until the afternoon. Assistant AG Sisko makes a bigger fool of himself than Reno did, but he also manages to take up a good two hours with his worthless monologue on a civil servant's duty to uphold the standards they are commissioned to enforce.

When George steps out of the meeting room, he is about to explode with frustration and exhaustion. Al Freeburger and Jim see their boss come out of the session and get up and walk over to see how it went. "Well, boys, we have to come back here tomorrow, 'cause that little carpetbagger is trying to filibuster those boys in there into finding something wrong with the way we do things."

Freeburger puts his hand to his chin and partially covers his mouth. "George, Belinda is in the cafeteria with Reno right now. I've seen her going in and out of offices around here all day."

Belinda Manning is George's ex-wife, whom Reno just tried to question him about. Three years ago, George caught her at home in bed with a Sheridan police lieutenant and divorced her over it. She decided to keep George's last name, because it made her feel important. The lieutenant was let go from the department and immediately moved away from Sheridan. George has remained single since then and does his level best to never be in the same place as Belinda. "So that's why that squirrelly bastard started bringing her up at the end. He's going to try to use her against me somehow."

Al sees an aide from the AG's office walking in their direction. He taps the sheriff's shoulder and points at the individual trying to get their attention. "Excuse me, Sheriff Manning, the attorney general would like a word with you and your two deputies in his office."

Al and Jim follow Sheriff Manning back to John Stalker's office, who motions them in to have a seat. Everyone can tell that the AG is upset about something and has been at his desk all day. He looks at all three and says, "George, Al, and—I didn't get your name, young man."

"Deputy Jim Edwards, sir."

The AG holds out his hand. "You're Carl Edwards's boy, aren't you?"

"Uh, yes sir, but he never mentioned he knew the attorney general of Wyoming."

"Son, I wasn't always the attorney general. The summer between my senior year in college and law school, I worked as a cabin boy on a passenger train for Burlington Northern. Your dad was my boss. That is one uncompromising man you have for a father. He was only a couple of years older than me, but he knew every square inch of that train from beginning to end."

Jim gets a big grin on his face and holds out his hand to shake the AG's hand. "You're damn right about the uncompromising part, sir. Momma always says Daddy was born with choo-choo steam in his blood."

The four men chuckle a little thinking about Jim's dad, and then the AG looks over at Manning. "That little bastard Reno just sent another request to me to file official charges against you for corruption, taking bribes, and dereliction of duty. Same as before, but now he says he has an eyewitness—your ex-wife, Belinda!"

"For crying out loud, John," Al replies. "That little hussy never told a truth her whole life." He then looks over at Manning and shakes his finger. "I warned you about her the first time I saw you two together. She's always bad news."

George just drops his chin to his chest and shakes his head back and forth. The AG gulps a little and as apologetically as he can, he tells the group that the real kicker in the whole mess is that his investigating team is headed up by the ex-Sheridan police lieutenant, Bill Arson, who had an affair with Belinda when she and George were married. George jumps out of his chair. "What the hell, John. So your team is useless to us!"

"Looks like it, George. He was in place before I got here, and my predecessor owed his family some favors. Getting rid of him right now would look a little biased for me."

Al's and George's faces are beet red, but Jim holds up his hand in an almost childlike gesture and says, "Sir, when I was studying criminal law at Sheridan Community College, they taught us that the state attorney general has the authority to appoint a representative law enforcement officer in a local county to represent him in an investigation of one of those county officials if he so desires. Is that true?"

"Well, yes, Jim, it is true, but I've known Al here as long as I've known George. Plus, Al is George's friend and top man in his department. Politically it would be suicide, and the governor would have me strung up for it."

Jim sits back with a crooked grin. "I wasn't thinking that you should appoint Al, sir."

John and George look hopefully at one another, then at Al. Al shrugs his shoulders. "He's the smartest damn deputy I ever trained. Plus no one knows him. Only been two years on the force. You ask me, he's perfect."

The AG looks over at the sheriff, who just nods his head. "Okay, it's settled. Since my new agent here will be investigating both of you, I'm going to have to ask you two to leave."

George's look of relief is manifested all over his face. Al just hits Jim in the shoulder and tells him not to let it go to his head.

For the next two hours, the AG and Jim go over everything they can on Reno's accusations against Manning. Before he leaves, Jim asks if he can see a manifest of all the expenses that Reno, Sisko, and Arson have charged to the state in the last six months. The AG calls down to Records, and even though it's almost 9:00 p.m., there is a clerk working who looks up all the forms and brings them up promptly.

Jim shakes the AG's hand, and before he leaves the AG tells him that he is now an agent of the Wyoming State Attorney General's office, and that means he has statewide law enforcement jurisdiction. He will make sure that all the proper authorities know that they are to give Agent Edwards their full cooperation in the investigation of Sheriff George Manning of Sheridan, Wyoming.

Later that night, Jim and Al are poring over all the financial details of each of the three men that have something to do with accusing their boss. There is a double ring on the room phone and Jim picks up.

The hotel front desk person says, "Deputy Edwards, we have a long-distance collect call for you from New York City. It's from Linda Edwards, and she says she's your wife. Would you like to charge the call to your room?" Jim tells her he would and then quickly notes the time on his wristwatch so that he can account for the phone call and pay Sheridan County back for the personal call.

"Jim, how is it going in Cheyenne? I hope Sheriff Manning is not in any serious trouble."

"Oh, it's a real setup, honey, but we're going to figure it out and clear him." He fills her in on some of the details, including his temporary appointment by the AG to investigate the matter.

"Oh, Jim, that better not be more dangerous than what you normally do. I want my husband alive and well by this Friday when I get home."

"You will, baby. How's Little Chunk?"

"Jacob's just fine. He misses his father. He caught wind of a new John Wayne movie called *The War Wagon* playing in a local theater here in the city. Now he wants you to take him to it. He got so excited that I spent half the day trying to find an older John Wayne movie playing on TV so that he could watch that. We finally got to see the last hour of *McLintock!*"

"That one's still my favorite. What do you get there, like eight whole channels on TV?"

Linda giggles. "Try thirteen, and eight on UHF."

"Geez, we barely get three in Sheridan and Story. I'm telling you, Linda, as soon as I make more money, we're switching to cable and that's final."

Linda giggles again. "Not until everything is settled with the house, and we start getting a good chunk of money put away for Jacob's college."

Jim tells Linda he loves her, gets Jacob on the phone and tells him the same thing, then hangs up. He pulls out a ledger from his pocket, looks at his watch, and marks the time he spent on the long-distance call. Al rolls his eyes. "You know that will be on the statement when we check out, right?"

"It never hurts to keep track for yourself. That's what Linda always says when it comes to spending money. Plus, my dad taught me to never let someone pay my bills when it isn't their business."

Al rolls his eyes again and says that if anyone in the department will ever wind up being rich, it's going to be Jim. No one else, including himself, has a lick of sense when it comes to money.

Around midnight, Jim nudges Al on the shoulder because he is sitting in front of the radio, half-asleep. "I think I found something pretty interesting."

Al looks up, grabs his warm beer to take a swig, and looks down at the paper Jim is holding. On it is a list of phone calls that Representative Reno made to Arizona that he charged to the state. He shows Al similar documents with Arson's and Sisko's names at the top that have phone calls to the same number. Arson also has made some to Mexico. All of them were turned in to the state for reimbursement. It's no secret that no one likes paying for long-distance phone calls and most government people usually turn in most of theirs, whether personal or not, to get reimbursed. Jim chuckles. "If these boys were as smart as they want everybody to think they are, they'd have paid for these calls themselves and we would never have seen them."

Al tells Jim that he will look into who those calls went to in the morning. Jim puts the paperwork away after making some notes on other angles he wants to check out the next day. After talking to Linda, he feels like he could go to sleep pretty easily, and he does.

The Next Day, State Capital

Since joining the sheriff's department, Jim started wearing a mustache. But that morning, knowing he is not going to be in uniform but still worried about someone recognizing him from the day before when he waited in the lobby all day for Sheriff

Manning, he shaves it off. He first stops by the AG's office and tells him his plan, which is approved, then makes a call to the state police office in the capitol building and heads to his next stop.

When he shows up outside the AG's investigation team's office, he does look quite different from the day before. He opens the door and steps into a large office with a door on the other end that bears the title *Chief Inspector Bill Arson* on the smoked-glass window. He shows his new identification badge to the receptionist, and points at the door of the director's office. The receptionist waves him over. He walks up and knocks while the three other men in the outer office and the receptionist nervously eyeball him.

"Who the hell is knocking on my door? Maggie, I told you to use the intercom system." Before the receptionist can respond, Jim reaches down, twists the knob open and walks into the office. Much to his delight, he walks in on a heavy petting session between Arson and George's ex-wife, Belinda. The embarrassed couple jump up from behind Arson's desk where Belinda was sitting on his lap. "How dare you barge into my office? Who the hell are you, boy?"

Jim knows he is really going to enjoy this. He remembers Arson from his days back on the Sheridan Police Department. He had a bad reputation for hassling teenagers who liked to cruise up and down Main Street on the weekends. One night, he pulled Jim over three times for no apparent reason other than he just did not like his old car. Arson gave him a bogus ticket for reckless driving that night.

When he went to court over the ticket, he pleaded no contest, which gave him the right to make a statement. Apparently, lots of parents had complained to this judge about Arson, and after he heard Jim's story, he threw the ticket out. There has been bad blood between them ever since. When Arson left Sheridan in disgrace four years ago, the senior class at Sheridan High threw a kegger party out at the quarries north of town to celebrate.

Jim reaches in his front jacket pocket and pulls out his brand-new state ID badge and card and shows it to Arson. "Inspector Arson, my name is Jim Edwards. I'm the AG's special agent appointed to oversee the Sheriff Manning investigation. I'm going to have to ask you for everything you have in this office on the sheriff, plus I would like to know if you're intimately involved with Mrs. Manning here, who happens to be Representative Reno's key witness against the sheriff."

Arson looks at the ID with an exasperated panic in his eyes, then focuses on Jim. "I know you, don't I? You're from Sheridan."

Jim explains that he is part of the Sheridan County Sheriff's Department, that he started two years ago, and that he was called in to investigate the allegations against the sheriff as per state law.

"This is ridiculous. I'm not going to share my case files with you. Hell, you work for the son of a bitch."

"Inspector Arson, my appointment gives me full authority over this case, you, and your staff. Do what I say, or I'll have you arrested for obstruction of justice."

"You go to hell, punk. I remember you now. You're that little bastard who got the judge to throw out one of my tickets. I'll see you in hell before you ever embarrass me like that again."

The whole time this is going on, Belinda Manning is doing her best to slide out the door behind Jim. He is having way too much fun to be intimidated or mad. He looks over at Belinda and asks her to sit down and then directs a jovial glare back at Arson. "I kind of expected you to act like this. So suit yourself." He puts his fingers to his mouth and lets out a little whistle.

Immediately, two Wyoming state troopers come into the main office, and Jim motions them over to Arson. "Arrest him and take him downtown and book him for obstruction of a criminal investigation and failing to cooperate with a state representative of the attorney general. When I think of or find some more stuff, I'll call you."

Arson, beside himself with indignation, hurls a bunch of useless threats in Jim's direction.

The two officers pull Arson's hands behind his back and handcuff him. At that point, Arson motions to Belinda to go over behind the desk and get something. Jim sees the gesture and goes over himself. He reaches down and picks up a little zippered bag that looks like a bank deposit bag. He opens it up and finds a big wad of hundreds and fifties in it, plus a note that says, "There's plenty more where this came from. Just keep that asshole Manning in Cheyenne as long as you can. Pack Leader."

Once he sees Jim read the note, Arson just hangs his head and slumps down, wallowing in self-pity as the troopers escort him out to jail. Before she can leave, Jim steps over to Belinda and motions for her to sit in the chair next to the receptionist's desk. He then looks at the rest of Arson's staff. "I kind of pride myself on being able to read how people feel about their boss, and I'm going to take a guess and say none of you really like that guy."

All at once, the four of them start telling him what a jerk he is and how they can't believe he ever got this position. Jim holds up his hand to quiet them down. "Who's the number two guy here?"

A man who looks to be in his late forties raises his hand. "That would be me." He holds out his hand and introduces himself as Donald Michaels.

Jim takes his hand and gives it a hearty shake. "Well, Mr. Michaels, looks like this is your office until the attorney general says different. All I ask is that you get all the case files pertaining to the Sheriff Manning investigation."

Michaels shrugs his shoulders. "That's just it—there really aren't any case files. Bill just came up with this cockamamie idea about a month ago when that girl showed up." He points over at Belinda. "He had just gotten back from a weekend getaway to Colorado, and he brought her in here with him. They'd spend all day every day together in there laughing and carrying on, telling the rest of us to just do our jobs and leave them alone. Sometimes, Assistant AG Sisko would come in and go right into the office and talk. The last time he was here, it was to drop off that satchel." He points to the satchel Jim has in his right hand.

As they are talking, another female Wyoming state trooper enters the office and asks Belinda to stand up. She puts her in handcuffs and escorts her out. Jim walks over to the phone on the receptionist's desk and dials the extension for the AG's office. He takes a few moments to explain to him what is going on. "Yes, sir, I believe we have enough to get Sheriff Manning's case thrown out. But there is a lot more going on here. I suggest you get the inquiry postponed for another day, and I should have some solid answers for you by tomorrow."

Jim hangs up the phone and looks over at Michaels. "The AG just told me that he can trust his own investigative team now that you're in charge, so he asked me to work directly with you for the rest of this investigation."

Michaels laughs. "Sounds good to me. How about you get Al Freeburger in here and the three of us will try to figure this mess out. Okay, Deputy, uh, Special Investigator Edwards?"

It doesn't take much to find Al. He is out in the main lobby of the capitol building with Manning, talking about how they just got news that the inquiry hearings were postponed until tomorrow. At first, they think that it's some kind of trick that Representative Reno is pulling, but Jim tells them both what's really going on. Jim looks over at Sheriff Manning. "Boss, I'm sorry that I can't invite you into the meeting, but acting AG chief investigator Michaels wants to meet with Lieutenant Freeburger and me right away."

Al smiles and pats Manning on the back. "Well, it's about time they put Michaels in charge of that outfit. Every time a new AG shows up around here, he gets passed over. I told him a couple of times to get out and go talk to the Feds. They would appreciate him a lot more than the state ever has."

Jim and Manning both look at Al a little confused. He just huffs and says, "You know, I never liked any of those college ROTC second lieutenants they sent me over the years. And especially when I was trying to keep a bunch of momma's babies from getting killed in combat. But back in Korea, Michaels showed some moxie and made us all proud. Hell, he had enough sense to listen to me and turned out to be a pretty damn good officer."

Sheriff Manning finally understands that Al is trying to tell both of them that he trusts this guy, and everything is going to be okay. "Okay, boys, I'm going back to the hotel to get some rest. Jim, you do your job the right way and look out for the AG's and the state's interests first. Al, I expect you to fill in the gaps and get us out of this crap and back home as soon as possible."

"I'm on it, boss, and don't worry about Jim—he's turning out to be a regular Dick Tracy. Hell, his little goody-two-shoes Boy Scout attitude about paying for all his personal phone calls blew this case wide open last night. All three of those dumb-asses charged the state with personal phone calls to Pack Leader and Grinder's camp down in Arizona, and Arson also made a call to a cartel safe house in Mexico."

Jim asks, "How do you know it was a cartel safe house?"

"Same way I know the Feds would treat Michaels better than the state. I was in the marines for thirty years, kid. I know a lot of government people."

Sheriff Manning holds up both hands, smiles at Jim, and tells him not to ask any more questions before he pisses Al off. Jim and Al say goodbye to the sheriff and head over to the AG investigator's office to meet with Michaels.

Jim brings Al back to Michaels's office. Before Al is halfway through the door, a very jovial Michaels is on his feet and over to the pair. He holds out a hand and gives Al a sideways grin. "If you think for one minute that I'm calling you *Lieutenant*, you're crazy. How's it going, Sarge?"

"Oh, I can't complain, kid. It's just that I do miss making sure you don't get yourself killed every day. But the Almighty did see fit to give me another one just like you." He slaps Jim on the back and they all have a laugh, although Jim's is a nervous one.

The three retreat to Bill Arson's former office and start to debrief about the case. The conversation goes on for about an hour, and they decide that Al and Michaels will pursue the phone calls, and Jim will try to track down Sisko and Reno today. Jim mentions that he saw Sisko yesterday and wants to check something out about his new car.

Frontier Chevrolet, Cheyenne, Wyoming

Jim is out on the lot of Frontier Chevrolet, a new car dealership in downtown Cheyenne, admiring the brand-new 1974 Pontiac Firebird on the lot. He remembers reading how GM is calling this "The Car of Tomorrow." He is about ready to open the hood when he hears a voice behind him say, "That ain't the eight-cylinder model. We only got two of those in and they both sold the same day. That there is the six-cylinder 250 cid 100-horsepower. The two we sold were the 175-horsepower models. We can order those, but this one here just got reduced from $2,800 to $2,650. The eight-cylinder is $4,800 now."

Jim knows that the six-cylinders are turning into a kind of flop, and GM is pressuring the dealerships to push the sales as much as possible. The salesman will probably get a higher commission if he unloads the six-cylinder models on the lot first. He looks at the salesman and can see the nervous desperation behind his big bravado sales pitch and decides not to torture the guy.

"Look, my name is Jim Edwards, and I'm an investigator for the Wyoming Attorney General's office." He pulls out his identification card and badge. "We're investigating some serious corruption in the State House of Representatives and the Wyoming State Capital bureaucracy. Now, you just sold two of the expensive ones. I need to know when and to whom."

The salesman is named Ryan, and he tells Jim that he's going to have to talk to the general manager. Jim agrees and follows him into the showroom, where he is led to an elevated set of desks. He and the salesman are greeted by an elderly, white-haired cowboy type with pearly white teeth. "Howdy, young man. I'm Bob, the deal maker. What can I saddle you up with today?"

Jim shakes the big guy's hand. The Sheridan Autos dealership is one of his favorite places to be around when he's not working for the sheriff's department. So he really understands the whole dealership dynamic. He doesn't want to raise any false hopes, so once again he pulls out his identification and badge and asks if there is someplace they can talk privately.

Bob's face goes from light to dark in the blink of an eye. He points Jim to the side and directs him to a conference room. Once there, they sit down, and Bob nervously asks, "So, what could the attorney general's office want with us today? Did Mr. Sisko and his friend do something wrong when they bought those two Firebirds last week?"

Intrigued, Jim takes note that Bob did not mention Reno's name, so he asks, "Did Sisko pay cash for both the cars, or did you sell them individually?"

Bob squirms in his chair a little and takes his palm and rubs it across his now sweaty scalp. "Investigator Edwards, ever since financing became easy with the fifty-six dollars down, fifty-six dollars a month deal GM came out with in the '50s, you just don't see folks wanting to buy cars outright. So when someone comes in with eight thousand in cash and wants to pay outright for a couple new cars, you tend to go for it. Hell, we don't have to share our commission percentage with the financing bank or nothing. It's a straight deal with a win for everybody."

Jim sits back and pulls out a newspaper clipping of Representative Reno being sworn in on the day of his appointment. "Is this the other man who came in with Mr. Sisko?"

Bob grabs the newspaper and a sullen look grows across his face as he realizes that a state representative intentionally withheld his identity from the dealership while Mr. Sisko purchased the vehicles. "Yes, that's him, but he didn't sign anything. Didn't even say much. Just fawned over the black Firebird and then pulled out some money and gave it to Mr. Sisko, and...oh shit."

Jim knew he had him now. "So, you sold both cars to Mr. Sisko but left one title blank and cut the deal that way, huh?"

Jim asks to see the finance manager of the dealership, and when he is brought back to the conference room, they show him the deal. Jim looks over the documents and sees that a letter from a notary in the state capital showed that the black Firebird was transferred over to Representative Reno through the State Transportation Department.

Jim has the finance manager make copies of the deal for his records and then says, "Guys, I know you're not running a crooked shop here. You just got slam-dunked by these two. But there is some serious fraud here that could come back to haunt you. Tell you what—Bob, you agree to come to the capitol building tomorrow and make a statement to the AG about how Sisko and Reno purchased these two vehicles, and I'll speak with him about granting your dealership immunity in this situation."

Bob and the finance manager readily agree to Jim's proposal. As Jim is leaving, Bob puts his hand on Jim's shoulder and asks, "Are we going to lose the deal and have to turn the eight thousand over to the authorities? That deal just put us in first place in our district for sales."

Jim laughs at the man's set of priorities, but after spending all that time at Sheridan Autos, he cannot help but feel a little compassion. "I kind of doubt it, but if everything goes like I think it will, those two cars will be confiscated and become the property of the state. That means they'll want to get rid of them as fast as possible. You could probably put a bid in for them with the state auction and get them back for a fraction of the original cost; then you could sell them again and make double the profit."

Bob's big, pearly whites again manifest themselves across his face as he pats Jim's shoulder. "I'll be there bright and early tomorrow. You ever decide to get out of law enforcement and go into car sales, look me up, kid. You have a knack for this stuff, and I'm not just spitting in the wind either. You're the real deal."

Jim returns to his truck and pulls out his pad. He makes a couple of notes then drives to his next destination, the Cheyenne County Jail. He introduces himself to the reception officers, and asks for an interview with two prisoners. "Excuse me, officer, where is the nearest pay phone?"

The middle-aged man points behind Jim. "Just through that door. You don't have to use the pay phone, Investigator. Just pick up the white phone next to the booth, and I'll have the receptionist put you right through."

"Thanks, officer. I appreciate it."

"No problem, always happy to help the AG's team."

As Jim heads to the door he mumbles to himself something about how he could get used to people treating him like this. "I'm here, Lieutenant, and I have all the info about those car purchases. I'm about to go in and talk to the prisoners. Say, what's the name of the cartel leader at the other end of that line down in Mexico?" Jim takes out his pen and writes down the name Renaldo Manerez, lieutenant in the Medellin Cartel. "Geez, are you sure about this? He's a very big player down there. If these two are connected to him, then we have a lot more problems than we ever thought."

Jim pulls the phone away from his ear as Al fills it with a few choice words about doubting his intel. When Al is done yelling at Jim, he tells him to wait until he gets there before interviewing Bill Arson and Belinda Manning. Jim hangs up and thinks to himself that technically he does not have to listen to Al right now because he's working for the AG; but after further consideration, he decides it's the most prudent thing to do, seeing how Al is his boss back home.

Forty-five minutes later, Al comes through the door with Donald Michaels, and they are arguing about a briefcase in Al's hand. "Al, you can't just take evidence like that and bring it to an interrogation without getting proper clearance. I don't have the authority to give that kind of clearance yet."

Al rolls his eyes and looks over at Jim. "Hey, Special Investigator Edwards, can I get your permission to use this evidence when we interview Tinkerbell and his girlfriend in there?"

Jim squints at Al and Donald and then looks down at the case. "Uh, sure, Lieutenant. What's in it?"

Al looks back and winks at Donald. "See, I know he has the authority, because it's his case and the AG gave it to him." He grabs a tag on the case with his free hand and holds it up so Jim can see it. He smiles and says to Jim, "See, it says 'Evidence.' Now let's go scare the hell out of those two assholes."

Bill Arson and Belinda are seated next to each other at an eight-foot table, handcuffed to two separate rings. Bill refuses to talk, and it's really starting to upset Belinda. When the trio walks in, she is yelling at him to talk or she's going to tell them what they want to hear.

The three men sit down with Al in the middle. Al says, "Now, Jim is the chief investigator here, so this is his interview, but I'll be asking most of the questions because he asked me to. Ain't that right, kid?"

Jim just nods his head.

Al winks at Jim then looks over at the couple and reaches inside his coat jacket. He pulls out the bank deposit bag they found in Bill's office yesterday. He opens it up, spreads all the money on the table, and holds up the note. "Now, you want to tell me what Pack Leader thought was worth twenty thousand dollars?"

"I never saw that before, Freeburger, and I have never even met Pack Leader." He points his chin in Belinda's direction and says, "How do you know if that money and note don't belong to her or Michaels over there? We were all in that office."

Belinda stands halfway up and yanks on her handcuffs and yells, "You bastard, I was standing right next to you down in Pueblo when that big biker made that deal and told you to work with Sisko and Reno. He made it with you, not me."

"Shut up, you stupid bitch. They're probably recording this whole thing."

Donald, who has been silent up until now, laughs and says, "Oh, Bill, you can be sure of that, and not just audio but video too." Belinda turns ashen and sits back down and buries her head in her arms.

Al continues. "So, you made a deal with Pack Leader down in Pueblo. Let me see—you two got back from Colorado a month ago, and you were there for a week. So let's just say that you had plenty of time to make a deal with him. Like I said, what could the AG chief investigator do for him that was worth twenty thousand dollars? Was it to help Sisko and Reno convict Manning on all those trumped-up charges?"

The couple remain stone quiet, except for Arson telling them that he wants a lawyer. Al laughs at their bravado, reaches under the table, pulls out a black leather briefcase and puts it on the table.

Bill Arson stares at the case in total disbelief. "How the hell did you find that?"

Al opens the case and turns it around so that the couple can see the contents. In it is a bunch of hundred-dollar bills, all stacked in neat little piles and fastened together with paper wrappers that have the amount of ten thousand dollars written on them. There are ten of them in the case, and in an envelope is a hand-written note that says, "This is the fifth of ten installments. Make sure that our operations in Casper and Cody go unhindered by any law enforcement in those locations. Keep me informed when you're ready to make the final move to secure our influence in the Wyoming law enforcement hierarchy. Renaldo."

Belinda is on her feet again and screams, "What the fuck is this shit? You have half a million dollars hidden away somewhere that you got from Pack Leader's and Grinder's supplier and you don't tell me shit."

Arson's look of defeat is wonderfully evident to all around him as he just leans back and says, "For crying out loud, Belinda, can't you ever keep your stupid mouth shut? Man, I thought banging almighty Sheriff George Manning's wife would teach him a lesson for not giving me Al's job here when I asked to transfer to his department. Turns out, all I did was do him a huge favor in taking you away from him."

Al is overjoyed by Arson's remarks. "You know, Bill, back during Nam I used to take wise-ass, know-it-all lieutenants like you out back by the latrine and teach them a lesson on respecting the one who keeps them alive. But hell, boy, you're right. When you started banging this whore and George found you, it was the best thing that could have happened for all of us. Now, why don't you just tell us all why you're on the take with Pack Leader and the Medellin Cartel's man? And how it seems that two different deals are going on here."

Knowing that everything they have said is already on tape, and that the evidence is stacked up against them, Bill and Belinda spill their guts. Bill tells them that after Grinder got himself thrown in jail, Renaldo Manerez approached him about helping with the new Cody and Casper operations. Then Pack Leader later paid thirty thousand dollars apiece to Sisko and Reno to pull Manning in for a hearing with the sole purpose of keeping him away from Sheridan for as long as possible. They brought Bill Arson in, because he could help Sisko control the AG during the proceedings. He was supposed to approach the two for the cartel and offer them thirty thousand dollars each but saw an opportunity to make more money and still give everybody what they wanted. So instead of him having to pay off Sisko and Reno, they ended up paying him off with the biker's money. So, he got to save sixty thousand dollars and make twenty thousand to boot.

Belinda glares angrily at Bill and then tells Al that when she found out from him that George was in trouble, she offered to help compound that trouble by testifying against him and saying that when she and George were married, she saw him take bribes from criminals.

Bill then reiterates that the Medellin Cartel approached him independently of the Wild Wolves' leader to help keep the heat off their fledgling operations forming in Casper and Cody. Jim takes note that Bill fails to mention the part about securing influence in Wyoming's Attorney General's office. Bill said that the Wild Wolves are supposed to go up to Sheridan County this spring and raise some hell, keeping all the attention up there and off the other areas. Pack Leader wanted the sheriff and his top deputy out of the way for a while to make that easier.

The whole time all this is going on, Jim is writing furiously in his notepad. He looks at both men next to him, sees they have no more questions, and says, "Okay, this all seems like the truth, but one thing is still bothering the hell out of me. Representative Reno and Assistant Attorney General Sisko are seemingly throwing their careers away for thirty thousand dollars. This case against Sheriff Manning didn't have a prayer in hell of going through to an indictment, let alone a conviction. It's a lot of money, but not enough to make that kind of sacrifice. I can see that the cartels are paying you off for the long term. Being the chief investigator for the AG and being on organized crime's payroll would be a valuable asset to them. But why sacrifice an assistant AG and a state representative? What's their angle after this is all played out?"

Bill solemnly says, "Who says they're being sacrificed? I was still supposed to approach them for Renaldo and offer a deal." He looks over at Belinda, who has lost all her bravado and just looks scared. She stares back at him and nervously nods. "If you want any more out of me, I'm gonna want a deal in writing and signed by the AG himself."

Two hours later, they are in the same room with Bill Arson and Belinda, but it is Attorney General John Stalker who is doing all the talking. "Bill, I never liked you, and I never trusted you. But you have some powerful friends, and when I came back to public life and took office, my hands were tied. Jim, Donald, and Al here say you want to make a deal. So, let's lay our cards on the table. We already have you for criminal conspiracy, taking bribes, fraud, and—what's this— tax evasion?"

Jim points his finger to the section of paper that the AG is reading from and says, "Yes, sir, I added that a little while ago. Seems Bill here has been on a buying spree. New speed boat, hunting cabin, and four-wheel-drive truck, to name a few. All paid for with cash and none of it reported for sales or income tax. In the long run, those charges will probably have the most teeth to them."

The AG shakes his head, laughs, and looks over at Al and chuckles. "You and Manning better hold on to this boy pretty tight, because I'm tempted to steal him from you two horse traders." He looks back at Bill and Belinda. "Bill, what could you possibly offer me that I don't have already?"

Bill has had time to collect himself and reestablish his composure. He leans back in his chair. "Your reputation and your career for starters. Then credit for taking down the biggest drug ring in the Rocky Mountains."

All four Wyoming law enforcement men are stunned by Bill's remarks. Jim puts his palms to his temples and exclaims, "I see it now! It all makes perfect sense, sir. You were the target all along. First, Sheriff Manning would be cleared and go home, then everybody was going to try and crucify Sisko and Reno. But Bill here was going to come to their rescue by implicating you in everything, including the chaos that's going to happen up in Sheridan!" Jim pauses, then looks at his notes and continues. "Of course, then the Medellin Cartel would have the two top men in the Wyoming Attorney General's office, and a state rep to boot. With you out, Sisko would be next in line."

Al is sitting there taking all this in. He holds his hand up to get everyone's attention. "Okay, that all seems pretty logical except for one thing. Why does this asshole get a million dollars from the Medellin that no one but he knows about, and the other two get thirty thousand apiece, and then Pack Leader and Grinder throw him another twenty? A million bucks is way too much money up front for just assisting Reno and Sisko in accusing the sheriff and then later implicating and taking down the AG here in a public scandal. That's more like a payoff for a high-profile assassination, not a trumped-up scandal."

The four men simultaneously look over at Bill Arson, who has just realized that something is going to come out that he really didn't want to reveal and thought he did not have to. Before he can speak, Al reaches under the desk and pulls out a manila envelope with some large pictures in it. Before he opens it, he looks over at the AG and says, "Mr. Stalker, have you ever met this woman before, and did you know she is George's ex-wife?"

John kind of squirms in his chair and clears his throat. "The answer to both your questions is yes. Ben Sisko and Bill here invited me out to supper a couple of weeks ago." He then looks gravely at Bill. "When Bill and Ben got up to go to the john, they left me alone with her. It didn't take her but twenty seconds before she was practically sitting in my lap flirting with me. I don't like to make a scene, but I'm a public figure, and I told her if she did not control herself, I would have her up on charges. I never told Bill, because after the way they got together, I figured there was no point. Why are you asking?"

Al takes out a couple of photographs that show Belinda sitting on John's lap and rubbing her hands on his chest while seated in a downtown restaurant. "I think these were going to end up on the front page of a couple of newspapers in the state." He then directs his attention to Bill. "I found these in your new hunting cabin this morning. The park service was kind enough to helicopter me up there and back. The pilot served with me in Korea and owed me a favor. Also found these."

He pulls out a pair of pants, a shirt, shoes, socks, and underwear. John grabs them and says, "These are my clothes, Bill! What the hell are you doing with them?" The AG is on his feet and practically breathing down Bill's neck.

Al stands up and gently puts himself between Bill and the AG, then reaches into the envelope and pulls out a letter. He hands it to John and says, "Do you recognize this, sir?"

John opens the letter and reads it. It says, "My love, I know that you are not responsible for the sickness that separated us in body and soul. As I lay you to rest, be confident that I will join you soon enough. Yours always, John."

The AG holds the letter in his hands for a few seconds as tears start to appear on his cheeks. He uses his sleeve to wipe them off and looks at Al with exasperation. "I wrote this three years ago when my wife, Lucille, died in the asylum. Her brain tumor hemorrhaged. I put this on her casket right after the funeral. How did anyone get their hands on it?" His eyes grow dark and his face turns bright red as he turns and wraps his hands around Bill Arson's throat. "You are former governor Arson's nephew, and it was a state funeral because Lucille was the head of the Department of Motor Vehicles, and you were there. You waited around until the end and took this out before it was buried with her. Why?"

Al and Donald spring to the AG and force him to release Bill. Jim is holding the letter, having picked it up when the AG threw it down. Jim looks at it very closely, then gazes at Bill with pure contempt as everything comes together for him. He walks around the table until he is next to Bill, then leans down and holds the letter in Bill's face. "You know, Bill, you have always been a real asshole. Back in high school we used to call you 'That Pig, Larson Arson,' because we all figured you were on the take. But this really cuts it to the bone. You were going to use this as a murder-suicide note. Those pictures were to prove that the AG here was having a secret affair with Belinda, but you were going to show that something went wrong. Probably something like she was cheating on him, he found out, and then killed her, then himself."

He looks at the AG's clothes and at Belinda, holds the clothes up in Bill's face, shakes them and says, "You were going to be wearing these when you killed her and then put them on the AG when you killed him. That's why the Medellin Cartel was willing to pay you a million bucks, because you were going to assassinate two people. Am I right?"

Everyone in the room is stunned at how Jim put all the pieces of the puzzle together and figured out what Bill was truly up to. They are all now staring at Arson with pure fury. He can see that all his secrets are out, and he has nowhere to turn but to spill his guts and hope for a deal. Before he can start talking though, Belinda lunges to the side, leans her head toward Bill's chest and manages to dig her teeth into it and draw blood. She thrashes around, violently screaming that he told her to flirt with the AG every chance she got to use it to blackmail him, and also to prove later that he was trying to set Manning up as a favor to her.

Al and Donald manage to get Belinda up and off Bill, and then take her out of the room. Within a matter of minutes, one of the jail nurses comes in and addresses Bill's wound. She looks over at Jim. "This man is going to need an antibiotic shot. Human bites can be infectious." Jim tells her to do whatever she needs to do.

As she leaves to get a doctor, Al and Donald return to the room and find Jim continuing the interrogation of Bill. "It was your plan to deal with the AG so that Sisko could take his place and you could arrange for someone to have the top two law enforcement people in the state on their payroll—that someone being Renaldo Manerez of the Medellin Cartel."

John Stalker has been sitting quietly in his chair since he found out the extent of Bill's plans. Back in his hands, he has the letter that he wrote to his wife. He takes it, folds it up, and puts it in his jacket breast pocket. He looks over at Jim, puts his hand on the young man's shoulder, and gives him a friendly shake. He looks over at Bill and says, "Renaldo Manerez couldn't buy me five years ago when my wife was dying of a brain tumor. He told me I would have enough money to get her the very best care in the world, but I refused."

He sighs, shrugs his shoulders, points at Bill, and looks at the other three in the room and continues. "He must have gotten to this little punk and has been working this angle since then. When Governor Arson was elected, he appointed someone else, and I went back to private practice. I only recently came back as a favor to our new governor until he could find a permanent replacement. Although he has told me numerous times that the job is mine, I never really planned to fully come back to office after my wife died. I just wanted to bide my time until the governor replaced me. But these guys all knew that Sisko was not what he was looking for and probably felt that they would have to force the issue with my death."

He stands straight up and holds out his hands in an attention-getting gesture, clears his throat, and says, "I will announce it first to you people in this room. I have reconsidered my desire to retire from public service and plan to spend the remainder of my days fighting for law and order in our great state of Wyoming. I will continue my duties as attorney general for as long as the sitting governor wishes me to do so. Gentlemen, please get a detailed statement from this man and have it on my desk by tomorrow morning. I will review it and decide what kind of deal will best benefit the interests of the citizens of our state. Thank you."

With that, John Stalker says goodbye and leaves the room. Jim and Donald are getting ready to take a statement from Bill when Al reaches inside the same bag that he'd pulled out the AG's clothing from, and puts a black pouch on the table with the name *Jerry* written across the front. He pulls out a note and twenty-five thousand dollars in hundreds and reads the note to everyone. "Hey Cuz, you keep the locals off those boys up on Casper Mountain and there is plenty more where this came from."

Al puts the note down and looks at Bill in the eyes and says, "Your cousin, Jerry Arson, is the night shift commander of the Natrona County Police Department. So, what's going on up there on Casper Mountain?"

The next day, the inquiry is dropped on Sheriff George Manning. The governor and Attorney General John Stalker meet with him to offer their apologies and compliments for doing such a fine job in Sheridan County. Both Assistant AG Ben Sisko and State Representative Martin Reno are arrested for corruption, receiving bribes, and conspiracy to frame Sheriff Manning. Bill Arson is charged with receiving and giving bribes, conspiracy to commit murder, and tax evasion.

Between Jim, Al, Michaels, and Manning, they establish that Bill Arson was only partially working with Sisko and Reno. The latter two were definitely on the take, working for Pack Leader and Grinder. But neither they nor Pack Leader were aware of Bill's connection with Renaldo Manerez. They advise the AG to keep the prisoners separate and especially keep a tight lip about Arson's connection to Manerez.

The AG then asks Sheriff Manning and his two deputies to investigate the details they found out about Casper Mountain and the Casper police lieutenant, Jerry Arson. He grants them full authority to investigate the situation and make arrests as they see fit. They leave for Casper in a state-owned Chevy truck around

9:00 in the morning and are at the Casper Police Department Headquarters by noon.

When Sheriff Manning meets with the Natrona County police chief, Rodney Small, he has a very interesting conversation about Lieutenant Arson. "I'm telling you, George, I had no say in the matter. Former governor Arson's office called me and said that if I want any more funding from the state for our department, I had to promote him to lieutenant and give him a shift command. The best day of my life was when that pompous SOB lost to our new governor. My contract says I can review promotions every year, and at the end of this one, he's back in a squad car or he's out."

"You know, Rodney, that's why I've stayed in the sheriff's department. We only get our funding from the county, so the state really doesn't have much say unless some idiot like Reno tries to get us on an ethics violation. Anyway, they have Bill Arson locked up in Cheyenne for a pretty big laundry list of crimes. He had a stash of cash that he was going to get to your lieutenant that we intercepted. He told him to keep the locals' attention off Casper Mountain. Got any idea what that might mean?"

"Well, I know he's got a cabin up there. And it just so happens that he took some vacation days to do some fishing, so he's up there right now."

Ten minutes later, George is out in the precinct lounge talking to Al and Jim about going up to Jerry Arson's cabin to see what he's up to. While the three are talking, Jim is watching Chief Small's door; and when he sees him come out of his office, he jumps up to intercept him. Al reaches over to stop him, but Manning pulls his hand down and tells Al to see what Jim wants.

Jim briskly walks up to the chief, holding up a hand to get his attention. "Excuse me, Chief Small. Deputy Jim Edwards, Sheridan County. Can I ask you a question?"

"Sure, deputy. What's on your mind?"

"Well, sir, we're heading up to Casper Mountain to investigate Lieutenant Arson, and I am just a little curious as to how someone who just made lieutenant last year can afford one of those cabins up there. You see, my dad looked into getting one on the lake up there a few years ago, and he found out how expensive they are. You can buy two or three up at Dayton-Kane near Sibley in Sheridan County for the price of one of those bad boys up there."

"You know, I never really thought about it. He started talking about his new cabin a couple of months ago. I guess we all just thought that his uncle helped him get it. But that makes no sense because after leaving office last year, Governor Arson declared bankruptcy and has been struggling since."

Jim has his notepad out and is taking down the info. He then asks, "What's the name of the realtor's office that sells those cabins? Do you know?"

"Yes. Yellowstone Realty over on South Duke Street."

Jim shakes hands with Chief Small and walks back over to George and Al. "I have an idea about the cabin, and I think we ought to go check with the realtor's office that sells those units up on Casper Mountain before we head up."

Jim explains that there is something off about Arson being able to afford one of those. When Al objects by saying that his cousin was ready to send him the twenty-five thousand dollars that they intercepted, Jim says that the payment looked like a first-time installment.

"How do you figure that, kid?" says Al.

"Because he said there's more where that came from. Usually you don't have to say that at the end of a regular payment."

Al takes his white cowboy hat off, scratches his head and looks over at George for something. George just winks. "I'm glad we got this kid away from the AG when we did. Something tells me we have a real detective in our department, and I think he would have scooped him up for himself. Let's check it out."

Yellowstone Realty, Casper, Wyoming

Neil Belkins is pretty proud of himself. Thirty years of renting and selling cabins and he is just about to finish one of the best deals of his career. He picks up the Moosehead ivory-handled mug he bought at The Old Faithful Inn in Yellowstone last year and takes a good gulp of some Irish Crème coffee with a tad of rum. Since it looked like spring would start out a little slow, he couldn't believe how lucky he was when those two lumberjacks from Washington State showed up in his office in March, and paid cash for his two most difficult properties.

The first was a cabin up on Casper Mountain. Although it was a beautiful little three-bedroom unit with a toilet, shower, and full kitchen, it was built on a site on Elkhorn Creek off State Route 505 that was right in front of a protected bear area in the park. The bears lived in some natural caves that were about five hundred yards behind the cabin. Whenever someone would rent the cabin, the bears would pay them a visit at night to rummage through the garbage for food. After a while, word got out and he could never rent the place, let alone sell it.

The next was a cabin in Cody. It was nestled five miles up the mountain off an old deer trail that you could barely get to with a small, four-wheel drive Jeep, on horseback, or hiking. And yet the two lumberjacks came in and laid $34,00 on the table and said they wanted both. It was like a dream come true. Not only did he sell the properties, but he got full commission, because he did not have to work through a bank or financial institution to help them finance.

He's just finishing up the final stages of the deed transfers when three men wearing sheriff's uniforms come in the front door of his agency. The middle one walks straight up to his desk and says, "Mr. Belkins, my name is George Manning. I'm the sheriff over in Sheridan County. My two deputies and I are here on behalf of State Attorney General John Stalker. We've been assigned to investigate a certain Natrona County police lieutenant by the name of Jerry Arson. Are you familiar with that name, sir?"

Neil feels the blood race to his temples as he almost coughs up the swig of coffee he just drank. He looks down at the deed and the name he was instructed to put both the mountain properties under. Then he just sighs. He has been in the business way too long to ever lie to a law enforcement agent. "I was just about to transfer deeds for two cabins to him—one up on Casper Mountain and the other over near Cody—as you were walking in." Neil fills them in on all the details.

Al asks, "Did you notice any tattoos on these lumberjacks, say…right on their shoulders or biceps? Like, for instance, a big black wolf or something?"

"I did notice some tattoos, but not wolves. Both the men who came to my office had some kind of Halloween scarecrow on their shoulders."

Al shakes his head and looks over at the sheriff. "The Scarecrows. I know that gang, George. Maybe twenty-five guys at best. Pure second-stringers. They usually stay in Utah and Idaho. The Wolves would waste them if they knew they were poking around here. And that's a hell of a lot of loot for them to be throwing around."

Jim interjects. "But it's nothing for the Medellin Cartel. If they are working for Renaldo Manerez, then they'll have all the funding they'll ever need. Sheriff, I think they're setting up a meth lab on Casper Mountain, and they're doing it behind that cabin, probably in those caves he mentioned."

Al rolls his eyes. "Are the bears helping them cook the stuff, kid? Sometimes your imagination gets away with you."

"No, but maybe they figured out how to deal with the bears."

"Kid, you and I both know that if anyone goes messing around with a bunch of bears living in a protected area, the park service is going to be all over them."

"True, but they could be paying off some rangers to keep things quiet."

Al starts to say something, but the sheriff raises his hand. "Hold on, Al, Jim might be on to something. You know how much the park service is being invaded by all those nature-boy hippies from the East. Hell, they might accept some meth as payment. We should just keep that in mind as we pay the good lieutenant a visit."

Jim adds, "Sheriff, I think we're going to need some backup before we head up there. If the Scarecrows have a police lieutenant and the park service in their pockets around here, who knows who else is helping them. There might be more Casper PD as well."

"Now hold on, Jim. I've known Chief Small since we were kids. He's so straight you could use him to level woodwork. There is no way he's on the take."

Al lets out a gasp of air, cocks his head, looks at Jim, and scowls. "Kid, you're just too damn good at this shit. It really bugs me! But George, I think he's right. I don't think Rodney is dirty either, but we can't take any chances. I know exactly who we can call for backup. Just leave it to me."

One hour later Jim, Sheriff Manning and Al are driving up State Route 505 with three Wyoming State Highway Patrol cars following them. Al managed to get ten patrolmen to follow them up to the cabin. Jim looks over at the sheriff and says, "Is there anyone in this state he doesn't know? How can you get ten off-duty highway patrolmen to drop everything and follow you up a mountain on a wild hunch?"

Manning shakes his head and chuckles. "Jim, you have to understand that Al here is also the highest-ranking noncommissioned officer in the Wyoming National Guard. All these boys are weekend warriors and don't want to get on his bad side. So, when he yells jump, they ask how high."

Al is driving the state truck as they lead their team to the cabin. Jim can see a very wicked grin on Al's face as Sheriff Manning explains his influence over the highway patrolmen following them.

Al decides to pull off the road about a half mile from the cabin. They get out of the truck, grab their gear from the bed, and walk over to talk with the patrolmen. Manning clears his throat. "The AG telefaxed a signed order to investigate Arson and his property, so this is all legal. We are authorized to use any force necessary to arrest any and all parties engaged in any illegal activity. My deputy Jim here thinks that a biker gang called the Scarecrows is setting up a meth lab in some bear caves about five hundred yards behind the cabin. Now, that's on park land, so it's the park service's jurisdiction. But our designation from the AG as special agents on his behalf gives us authority even there. We're going to hoof it from here. So I'll turn it over to your beloved Sergeant Major Freeburger to set this up."

Al gets a huge smirk on his face and bellows out, "Okay, boys, this is how we're doing it. Deputy Jim and I will take point. The sheriff and one of you will be right behind us. The rest of you will walk in groups of two. Stay sharp and stay quiet. We want to surprise them."

Fifteen minutes later, Al and Jim are crouched behind a couple of rocks about twenty yards in front of the caves, and what they are looking at proves all of Jim's suspicions to be true. There are about a dozen men around the area. One is off-duty Lieutenant Jerry Arson of the Natrona County Police Department. There are also a couple of park rangers and the rest look like bikers, except none of them are dressed in the usual Levi's and sleeveless shirts or Levi jackets. They are wearing white T-shirts and Dickies work pants like northern lumberjacks do.

Al points out to Jim that on a couple of the bigger guys, the shirts are so stretched across the shoulders and arms that you can see the scarecrow tattoos. As they are watching them set up an obvious meth lab inside the cave, Jim directs Al's attention to an argument going on over at the far side of the camp. He looks back and motions Sheriff Manning and his partner to follow them over to see what's going on. As they leave, two highway patrolmen take their place behind the rock.

When they get there, they are able to see a very large, heavily barred cage with two brown bears and several cubs inside, all sleeping, as a group of men are arguing with the park rangers.

"Dude, you never said anything about drugging the bears," says one of the park rangers.

A large, red-headed man with a thick beard and mustache answers. "Just how in the hell did you expect us to control them without killing any of them? The vet we got the drugs from said none of them will be permanently hurt. It's the same stuff they use in Hollywood when they make movies with these things. He said if we give them enough, they can be led around on leashes. When somebody comes around, we'll just let a couple loose and they'll scare them away. Besides, man, you two been paid three times your yearly salary. Quit crying."

"When in the hell am I going to get my first paycheck? It's been almost two months," says Jerry Arson as he joins the group.

"You mean besides having that cabin just handed to you on a silver platter? That baby cost twenty thousand dollars. The other one up in Cody cost fourteen thousand dollars. I'd say they're pretty good first-time pay."

"Oh, sure, they're in my name, but I can't sell them and pocket the money. I want cash, guys, not custodianship of a couple of mountain cabins."

The big red-headed biker is getting annoyed and sticks his finger in Arson's chest. "Look PIG, your fucking cousin is sending you twenty-five thousand dollars sometime this week. You get another twenty-five thousand dollars every four months for as long as we can keep this operation going up here. So just chill before I put you to sleep with my fists."

Al stands up and shouts, "It does my heart good to tell you that your money is not gonna make it. But your consolation prize is maybe you and your scumbag cousin can share a cell in the state pen."

With that, Al, Jim, Sheriff Manning, and ten highway patrol-men armed with shotguns step forward. Al has them in a semicir-cle around the cave entrance and the criminals are so completely taken by surprise that none of them even attempt to respond, except for their red-headed leader, who turns in Al's direction and goes for the .45 caliber 911 on his hip. Al sees the move and quick-draws his .357 duty pistol and shoots the man in the groin area. He falls over sideways, screaming and holding his crotch.

Sheriff Manning then hollers, "Everyone else on your knees with your hands on your head!" He orders his deputies and the highway patrolmen to begin cuffing the rest of the people at the meth lab site.

Al and Jim go over to the area where the biker leader was shot. While Jim is cuffing Jerry Arson and the two park rangers, Al bends down to look at the biker's wound. The biker has both hands on his crotch and is almost crying when he spurts out, "You stupid pig, you almost blew my dick off!"

Al smirks as he pulls the biker's hands away to inspect the wound. "Shit, kid, I'm sorry. I was aiming for your hand. I'm just getting old. Can't see like I used to."

Two hours later, the highway patrol vans and an ambulance are loading up prisoners to be taken to the Natrona County hospital and jail for arraignment. Sheriff Manning, Al, and Jim are standing together with some highway patrol brass discussing the case.

A lieutenant from the highway patrol has his report book out and is taking down the info that Manning and his deputies are giving him. He can't help but chuckle when he says, "Sheriff, this is the biggest meth lab bust since the one you did up in Story two years ago. It's going to be a very nice feather in our department's cap. Hope the locals don't cause any waves about jurisdiction."

"I wouldn't worry about Chief Small. He'll have his hands full investigating his department when news gets out about his night shift lieutenant and the park rangers. Things around here are going to be as low-key as possible. I was acting on behalf of Attorney General Stalker anyway. He wants us to head over to Cody next and check out the other cabin."

"Sounds like the AG doesn't want you back home running your own department right now, Sheriff."

"Nah, that's not it. We're old friends and when they cleared me of all those bullshit charges Reno trumped up, I said I'd help. Besides, I've got this Dick Tracy deputy over there that the AG took a shine to. Hell, I'm anxious to get him home before someone else offers him a better deal than I can. Even Al likes him, and you know that takes some doing."

As they are talking, two very scared park rangers are paraded past them with their hands cuffed. Everyone can hear them yelling.

"When Sarah hears what we let happen to those bears, she'll never speak to me again."

"She won't be able to speak to you anyway after she OD's on all that pure meth you gave her last night."

"Will you shut up!"

The sheriff shakes his head and laughs. "Those two park rangers just came out here last year. They both graduated from some eastern college in forestry and wanted to come out and save the Rockies from all the evil men trying to ruin them."

"Never knew a hippie to turn down some good drugs. Those guys are going to be very uncomfortable in county lockup. Then the state penitentiary is going to seem like hell to them."

As Al and the sheriff are talking, one of the patrolmen waves Jim over to his squad car. "Hey, I got dispatch on my two-way. They're saying there has been some pretty nasty stuff that went on in Sheridan County last night. Rape, murder, and a couple of kids got beat up really bad."

Jim runs up to Sheriff Manning and Al to tell them what he just heard. The sheriff stares at Al and Jim. "I need to get to a phone now," he says. All three hop in the truck and head back to Casper.

When they get back to Casper, they head over to the highway patrol office for that area and the sheriff gets on the phone with his office. He finds out about the attacks in Story by the canyon and at the Sheridan graveyard. It's 4:00 p.m. and the shuttle flight from Denver to Sheridan is due to land in Casper at 4:30 p.m. The sheriff gets on the phone with someone at the Casper airport and reserves three seats. Sheridan is only a two-and-a-half-hour drive from Casper, but the flight is twenty minutes, and at this point all three want to be there yesterday. A highway patrolman tells Jim that they'll get the state truck back to Cheyenne by tomorrow, which he enthusiastically thanks them for.

The highway patrol gets them to the airport at 4:20 p.m. and they literally run through the outside gate of the airport landing field and over to the little twenty-seater twin engine turboprop and get in line to board. When the trio steps onto the plane, Jim's heart goes straight to his throat. There in the second row is his wife, Linda, and their son, Jacob. There are two seats on one side of the aisle and one seat on the other. Linda and Jacob are in the duo and a rough-looking middle-aged man is sitting in the one across from them. Jim immediately asks the man if he can sit next to his wife and son. At first the man refuses, but then looks at Sheriff Manning and Al behind Jim and gets up and lets Jim have the seat. Jim reaches over, grabs his son and kisses his wife. "Hey there, Little Chunk. You been a good boy?"

Jacob giggles and wraps his arms around Jim's neck. "Daddy, I watched three John Wayne movies with Mommy. It was cool."

Jim looks over at Linda and raises one eyebrow. She just rolls her eyes. "I had to do something to keep his mind off missing you."

He reaches over and pats her knee. "I totally forgot that you were flying home today. We had to catch this flight because some really bad things happened last night in Story and Sheridan, and the sheriff wanted to get there as fast as possible."

Trying to have a decent conversation with his wife is turning out to be quite a challenge because Jacob is jumping up and down in his dad's lap and clapping his hands. Finally, the stewardess tells everyone to strap in because they are about to take off. He hands Jacob back to Linda, and she gets him and herself settled.

As the plane takes off, Jim reaches over and grabs his wife's hand. He does not let go of it until the plane lands in Sheridan twenty-five minutes later. When they get off the plane, two sheriff's cars are waiting just outside the runway. The sheriff and Al get into one, and Jim, Linda, and Jacob hop in the other, and they take off. The mayor wants to meet with Sheriff Manning, the chief of police, and Al right away. They tell Jim to get his family home and then meet them later at the sheriff's department.

Chapter Seven
Cartel Retaliation

Altar Municipal Police Station, Mexico

Renaldo Manerez sits at the Altar chief of police's desk and fumes as he contemplates his latest reports on his Rocky Mountain operations. Getting that phone call from the Cheyenne, Wyoming, law firm representing Bill Arson informing him of all the trouble that he was in, and that his worth to the Medellin Cartel has just became null, was bad enough. Then came the news that his Casper Mountain meth lab got shut down before it could even begin. He has a pretty good idea what the problem is. Pack Leader and Grinder saw behind his scheme and decided to pull out some insurance of their own by bribing the Wyoming assistant AG and State Representative Reno, people who he himself was going to reach out to through Arson. But Arson got greedy and accepted money from the bikers while pretending to work with the government officials for them.

They all thought that getting Sheriff Manning and his most annoying deputy out of Sheridan for a while would help them get out when it got too hot. The whole thing blew up in their faces when the ones they thought they got rid of started investigating them in Cheyenne. Renaldo is dumbfounded that this puppy of a deputy, Jim Edwards, was so competent in his ferreting through the layers of deception that he ended up uncovering almost everything and implicating everyone. Fortunately, he was able to close down and move his Cody operation before those three could get to that one as well.

Now he finds himself moving all his business dealings away from the Altar Municipal Police Station because those idiots in Wyoming tried to charge their phone calls to the state as business-related—yet another detail uncovered by the deputy who beat up Grinder. As he sits at the desk he will soon be vacating, he is dreading his next call. But he still picks up the phone and dials an unpublished, long-distance phone number in Colombia, South America.

Señor Escobar sits in his 1964 Rolls Royce enjoying an exquisite Cuban cigar and a glass of his finest Caribbean brandy when his radio car phone rings. He immediately surmises who is calling him and answers. "Renaldo, I have been expecting to hear from you for a while now. I have to tell you, I am not pleased with how our northwest operations are proceeding in the United States."

"I assure you, Señor Escobar, that I am doing everything in my power to salvage the situation and cover your losses."

"Oh, Renaldo, if I thought for one moment that any of this disaster was your fault, you would not be alive right now. Those bikers you want to work with have always been loose cannons, but this sheriff and his deputies are intriguing. Whoever would have thought that such law enforcement competence could be found in the Wild West."

Renaldo breathes a sigh of relief and asks how they should proceed from this point.

"I still believe that the biker gangs can help us. I want you to prove to them that we are their greatest allies. Start smuggling additional Wild Wolves into Sheridan County to help Pack Leader and Grinder. We are going to turn this whole situation up there into a war between the bikers and local law enforcement.

Hopefully, the sheriff and his two deputies will be killed in the ensuing battles. When it gets the hottest, we will help the rest of the gang travel up there to rescue their friends. The Wyoming governor will have no choice but to call out the National Guard. That will be the end of Pack Leader and Grinder, but we will appear to the rest of the biker gangs as business partners who stand by their friends. Then we can rebuild our operations there and become even more powerful than before."

"What about Arson, Reno, and Sisko? They're all at the county jail in Cheyenne. Their testimony could hurt us."

"I have a young man coming your way today who will take care of these problems. I would have preferred to use the Chameleon, whom you met a few weeks ago, but he will be unavailable for a while. The man I am sending is young but quite talented. His name is Anthony. His English is very good. Just get him to Cheyenne. He'll take care of our three friends."

Renaldo hangs up the phone after thanking his boss. He looks up and sees his son, Maximillian, standing in the door waiting for him to finish. "There is a big Mexican out here named Anthony. He says you are expecting him."

"Send him in."

Maximillian goes out and comes back in with a large, muscular man in his early twenties. When they enter through the door he can't help but notice the natural animosity between the two young men, like two young bulls standing too close out in the pasture when there are a bunch of cows in heat. His son has already proven to him that he can kill when needed, but if this one comes straight from Escobar with orders to kill, he must be exceptionally good at his job. He tells Maximillian to wait out in the other office while he talks with the Medellin cartel hitman.

"I just got off the phone with Señor Escobar. You are to be given transportation to Cheyenne, Wyoming, where you are to take care of some loose ends that threaten the cartel's operations in that area. What else do you need from me?"

The Medellin man's face is unreadable, but Renaldo can see that there is a hint of annoyance in his eyes. He replies, "Only that when I am done you get me out of there as soon as possible. I don't like being around all those gringos."

Next Day, Cheyenne, Wyoming

Anthony is provided with a very good fake ID and other papers that show he is a migrant farm worker born in southern Texas. He shows up at the Cheyenne, Wyoming, bus depot the next day. He gets off the bus and immediately heads to the restroom where he finds an empty stall with an "out of order" sign hanging on the door. He pulls the sign down and goes inside.

When he pulls the lid off the tank part of the toilet, he finds a large plastic bag. He carefully pulls it out and retrieves the contents. He finds a Smith & Wesson .45 caliber semiautomatic pistol with three extra clips and an undergarment holster, one thousand dollars in tens and twenties, and pictures of his three targets. He puts the gun, clips, holster, money, and pictures in his duffel bag. He then opens a small bag and finds a half-ounce container of clear liquid and a small syringe. He reaches down and opens up a part of the back of his heel on his left shoe and inserts these items, then heads out to find a newspaper.

After thoroughly looking through the paper and asking questions of some local Mexican-Americans, he finds out that Sisko and Reno have posted bail and are at their residences in the area. Arson, however, is still being held in the local jail because his judge would not grant him bail.

He then asks the same people to name the bar in town with the biggest attitude against Mexicans. To his surprise, they really can't come up with a place that is a no-fly zone for Mexicans, but they suggest the Rustlers Bar on Main Street. The people tell him that they've had a lot of fights break out there lately. He asks for directions and finds out it's only a few miles away, so he decides to wait a couple of hours and then walk over.

On his way to the bar, he finds a park that is deserted and walks over to a hand-push merry-go-round for children. He takes one good look around to make sure he's alone and then gets down and crawls under it. He takes his gun, the pictures, and most of the thousand dollars and stuffs them under some leaves and debris, gets out, brushes himself off, and heads for the bar.

It's 9:30 p.m. and Anthony has been pretending to drink a lot more whiskey than he has actually consumed while the whole time looking for an opportunity to meet his need. He finally sees it in the form of a beautiful young cowgirl sitting on the lap of a big cowboy with a "don't mess with me" look on his face. He finishes off the shot of whiskey he is drinking and then orders another. He grabs the drink from the bartender, takes a couple of sips, and lets the rest spill on his chest and shirt. He looks over at the couple, stands up, and wobbles in their direction.

Anthony is not a small man. At six foot, three inches and 235 pounds, he has the look of a heavyweight wrestler. But when he slovenly approaches the couple and grabs the girl's hand and asks her to dance, the big cowboy stands up and shows just how big he is. Anthony's head barely comes under the chin of the cowboy as they stand facing one another.

The big man leans down and smells Anthony, smirks, and gives out a big "Whew!" He puts up a forestalling hand and says, "Look, pal, you've had one too many. My wife wanted to go out tonight. I'm not looking for any trouble, but she ain't dancing with you."

Anthony grabs the man by his shirt and threatens to knock his big ass on the floor if he does not get out of his way.

He wakes up two hours later in the Cheyenne County Jail.

He knows that getting to Arson is going to be difficult because he's a high-profile prisoner and Anthony is basically in the drunk tank. But as luck would have it, he sees that he is in a cell with other men lounging around, nursing varying degrees of hangovers. He looks around the cell and finds another large man who almost fits the description of the one who knocked him out at the bar. It is not the same man, but he quickly figures that he will do for his purposes. Without so much as a warning, Anthony jumps up and attacks the large man. As he jumps on top of the man, he starts to pummel him with his fists and yells, "You bastard, I just wanted to dance with her. I'm going to kill you!"

At first, the man is so surprised that he is paralyzed by Anthony's attack. He barely manages to get his arms up to guard his face as this crazed, drunken man rains down blows. Eventually he rolls to one side, shifting Anthony off him, and then he stands up. He looks down at the half-crazed man on his knees in front of him and kicks him in the chest, knocking him on his back. "Are you out of your stupid mind, *cabrón*? They are going to put you in the main lockup now. You won't even see a judge for a while."

Anthony sits up, grabs his head with both hands, and vigorously rubs his eyes and head with his hands. "Amigo, I am so sorry. I woke up and thought you were the guy at the bar who knocked me out. I can't stay here for a week. I have to be at the watermelon fields in Utah in two days."

The cell door opens up and four uniformed county jail guards come in. "You should have thought of that before you started getting drunk and picking fights on your layover for the next bus, buddy," one of the guards says. They stand Anthony up and take him out to go to the main lockup.

As Anthony hoped, he is paraded right by the general lockup and put in a cell marked "Maximum Security." He has done his research before coming to Wyoming and was able to find out that the county jail had only two max security cells sitting next to each other on the far side of the general population compound. Much to his delight, sitting in the other cell that he saw through the bars before the guards put him in is the attorney general's now former head investigator, Bill Arson. The guards put him in the cell and tell him that he will be fed later that evening. He waits until no one is near and walks to the front and leans sideways on the bars right next to the wall that separates him and Arson. "Renaldo Manerez sends his regards, Bill Arson."

There is a cold silence for about ten seconds before he sees a couple of hands come through the other set of bars and clasp together. "Are you here to kill me?"

"That depends on you, *hombre*. You took a lot of Medellin money and accomplished nothing. Now it looks like you can really cause some problems for us."

Bill feels the cold icicles start to prick the back of his neck and spine as fear builds up in his lower gut. "What can I do to stay alive?"

"For starters, you can give our money back. That always has a positive impact on Señor Escobar. Then you can tell us everything you've told these gringos." Bill tells him that he can tell Anthony where to find what's left of the five hundred thousand that he has already received. The words "what's left" are not lost on Anthony, and he asks what happened to the other part. Bill tells him that he spent almost eighty thousand already, and a hundred thousand more was confiscated by the AG.

"So, where is the three hundred, twenty thousand dollars then, *hombre*?" While he waits for Arson to answer, he slowly bends down and pulls the small package out of his shoe that was tucked under the heel insert. He delicately unwraps it and places the contents—a small needle, syringe, and vial—in his left hand.

He then inserts the needle into the top of the vial, fills the syringe with the clear liquid, and puts the vial down.

Finally Bill responds. "I hid the cash in the back seat of Belinda's car. She was always snooping through my apartment looking for anything she could find, so I figured the best place to hide stuff from her was with her. Besides, if it was ever found, I figured I could make a case that I knew nothing about it."

Anthony raises an eyebrow and half smiles. "That was actually a good move on your part, Arson." He is almost sorry for what he has to do next, but orders are orders. He reaches his right hand through the bars and in Arson's direction. "We have your lawyer working very hard to get you out of here on bail. If the money is there like you said, when you're out we will get you down south of the border. Señor Escobar always has work for intelligent people."

Bill lets out a big huff of air and a sigh of relief as he reaches over to shake the man's hand. When their hands meet, Anthony yanks his hand and arm over to him, sticks the needle in Arson's wrist and injects the contents. Anthony does not like poisoning his targets, but he knows that this will be his only shot. So he brought enough Angel's Breath with him from Colombia to kill a two-hundred-pound man.

The drug does not kill instantly, but it does render its victim senseless within a matter of seconds. Arson will not know where or who he is up to the time the drug does claim his life a few hours from now. Anthony continues to hold on to Arson's hand until he feels it go limp. An almost disembodied voice comes from its owner. "Where am I? Who has my hand?"

Anthony smiles as he gently releases his grip. "You must have gotten pretty drunk last night, buddy. You got up to go to the bathroom and slipped into the bars. I caught your hand when it came into my sight. You need to go back to bed and sleep it off, so they can release you later."

"Jail? What did I do to get into jail? Oh, you said I got drunk. That must be why I am so dizzy. I think I will lie down."

Anthony waits until he hears Arson lie down and then goes over to the toilet in his cell. He takes the needle, syringe, and vial and flushes them down. Then he thoroughly washes his hands and arms and sits back down on his cot. Three hours later as the guards are serving the two inmates their supper, they notice that Bill Arson is unresponsive. The prison doctor is called to the cell. He examines Arson and pronounces him dead.

Two days later, Anthony is brought before the judge and fined eight hundred dollars. Because they thought he was a migrant worker from Texas and really could not afford the fine, they give him the option to make payments. He had one hundred dollars on him when he was arrested, so he put that down and was released with an order to make good on the fine within six months or a warrant would go out for his arrest.

Anthony knew the value of having an established fake identity in a region. Having a drunk and disorderly on his record in the States would only work to legitimize the persona for later use, but having a warrant out on that same identity would be a hindrance. He goes directly to the merry-go-round in the park and gets the rest of the stashed cash and equipment, then goes back to the courthouse the next day and pays off the rest of the fine, saying that relatives loaned him the money.

After visiting the courthouse, he goes to a telephone book and looks up the addresses of Belinda Manning, Ben Sisko, and Martin Reno. Though the two men had only a loose connection with the Medellin Cartel by way of Pack Leader and Grinder, his orders are to kill both. He received no orders from his boss about Belinda, but he knows he can justify her death. More importantly, Anthony thinks he might be able to make a little side profit and have some fun in the process. When he gets to Belinda's house around 9:00 p.m., he sees that there is a light on. He hoped she would be out on bail by now, like the others, and the light would seem to prove that true.

The fact that Señor Escobar never told him to try and get the bribe money back from Arson pleases Anthony to no end. He has ambitions of his own, and only two things can ensure him accomplishing them—muscle and money. He is dead set on getting more of the latter tonight. It still irks him to no end that his boss would pay that creepy Russian they call the Chameleon millions to hit high-profile targets and only pay him a small fraction of that amount to do the same. So every chance he gets, he takes a little extra cash for himself. He knows that someday he is going to have enough to break out on his own, and being one of the best hit men in South America meant he could defend himself very nicely.

The next day, Belinda Manning is found dead in her car on the outskirts of Cheyenne. Authorities say she was raped and then murdered. The back seat of her 1968 Buick Skylark was cut up and torn out. No one knows why. Also, that same evening both Ben Sisko, the former assistant attorney general, and Martin Reno, the former state representative, are found dead in their homes, their necks broken.

At the bus station in Phoenix, Arizona, Anthony Santiago gets off the Greyhound that carried him from Cheyenne, Wyoming. He has two bags in his hands—one containing all his personal and professional belongings, and in the other about $350,000 that no one knows he has.

Chapter Eight
Things Get Ugly

Story, Wyoming

It has been six days since the trio got back to Sheridan County. The panic and fear in the area is as thick as pea soup because no one knows where the bikers came from and where they went. No gangs have been spotted within a hundred miles of Sheridan, and most of Sheridan County law enforcement personnel are really spooked. Sheriff Manning and his associate chiefs of police in Sheridan and Ranchester have all their patrolmen on double shifts. Even the Wyoming Highway Patrol have units all over the place. There is talk about the governor calling out the National Guard if things escalate.

Little Goose Canyon and parts of Kendrick Cemetery in Sheridan are closed down and sealed off, pending crime scene investigations. Jim, Al, and Sheriff Manning, along with a myriad of local and state law enforcement people, are all over both scenes, trying to piece together what happened. Al Freeburger has plans to drive up to the Billings, Montana, hospital in a couple of days to talk to the brother and sister who were attacked in the cemetery. Sheriff Manning had Jim go with him to Sheridan Memorial Hospital to talk to the one survivor from the Little Goose Canyon attack. By the sixth day back, every one of them has put in almost eighty hours of work and none has any solid leads on where the bikers are or how they are getting around.

It's about 7:00 a.m. and Jim has just got off the phone with Al Freeburger who told him that Belinda, Sisko, and Reno are all dead. Sisko and Reno were clearly murdered. An autopsy is being performed on Arson to determine why he was found dead in his cell earlier that week. The Cheyenne PD has no real leads into any of the cases, but the AG asks his new chief investigator, Donald Michaels, to help with the investigation. Jim knows that if anyone can figure out what happened, Michaels can.

After Jim hangs up the phone in the living room, he pats Thunder on the head. He walks into the kitchen where Linda and Jacob are having breakfast. He smiles and stretches as he tries to rub the sleep out of his eyes. He just got off patrol at midnight the night before after pulling a double shift and he's getting ready to do the same thing again today.

"If Al could have waited until you checked in at the sheriff's department, you would have gotten another hour of sleep, honey," Linda says. She kisses her husband and starts to prepare him something to eat. As usual, Jacob has more energy than six baby bear cubs, demonstrated by the fact that as soon as his dad sits down, he stands up and jumps out of his highchair into Jim's arms. He takes the forty-plus pounds of muscle and bone that is his son, lies him down on his back on top of his knees and starts to torture the boy with what Jim calls "The Five Fingers of Tickle."

Linda walks over with some pancakes and eggs on a plate and stares at her two juveniles. "I am not giving this to you until you put him back in his chair. I just painted this kitchen the day after we got back from New York, and you are not ruining it."

Jim is hungry, and Jacob knows when his mommy is serious. Jim helps his son back into his highchair and then starts to dig in.

Thirty minutes later, there is a knock on the front door. Jim gets up and walks to the front of the house. Before he gets to the door, he grabs his utility belt and sidearm and straps it on, because he knows he has to leave for work right away. When he opens the door, two men in their early thirties are standing on his porch. They have the look of tourists, so he looks around his driveway and sees a VW van with Florida plates.

The first, a dark-haired man wearing a denim, long-sleeve cowboy shirt and a pretty new looking white cowboy hat, smiles and says, "Excuse me, Deputy Edwards, my name is Seth Brown and my buddy here is Todd Wilkinson. We're here with a bunch of friends on a ten-year college reunion cross-country trip. We noticed that the canyon is all closed off and were wondering if there was any other place we can go fishing around here?"

Jim smiles as he looks both men in the eyes. "Guys, I'm a sheriff's deputy, not a park ranger. The canyon is closed off because there was a murder up there last weekend, and they're still going over the crime scene."

The blond-haired man, dressed much like his friend, steps up. "A murder? Good gawd, that's awful. Did you catch anyone yet?"

Jim steps out onto the porch and closes the door behind him. The presence of his Taurus .357 duty pistol on his right hip feels strangely reassuring as he continues the conversation with these two tourists. "No real leads yet, but we're pretty sure it was biker-gang related."

The front door opens as Jim is speaking and Linda steps out with Jacob nipping at her heels. Thunder is right behind Jacob and he gives a growl at the two strangers as Linda scoots him back in. Jim finds that interesting, because Thunder is just about the friendliest dog he has ever owned.

Linda gets the door closed and is holding a lunch pail. "You forgot your lunch, honey." She hands him the lunch pail and looks at the two men. "Hi, I'm Linda Edwards. Are you boys working a case with my husband?"

Seth steps forward. "No, ma'am, we're tourists. We were just wondering where we could go fishing since the canyon is blocked off now."

She looks over at her husband and can tell that he is annoyed by the fact that someone is coming to him with a question like that. Linda laughs and says, "Jim, the park rangers are all up by Bear Lodge for a week on some type of park land surveying exercise. The station is closed right now, so that's why they came here. Your squad car is right out front." She then looks back at the two men. "You know, there are some pretty good fishing holes on the Little Goose Creek just around Ranchester. Also, if you go over to Dayton and hike far enough back into Tongue River Canyon, you might just get a northern pike on your line."

The blond tourist named Todd puts on his best smile, eyeballs Linda from head to foot, steps forward and takes her hand and kisses it, then demurely says, "Thank you very much for that intel, Mrs. Edwards. We'll take you up on that advice."

By now, the hairs on the back of Jim's neck are standing straight up and he feels a cold prickle going up and down his spine. Thunder is at the window next to the door, and he is giving a low, dangerous-sounding growl. Jim forcefully releases Todd's grip from his wife's hand and steps between the two. With an ice-cold stare that could freeze an erupting volcano, he bores straight into both men as he tells Linda and Jacob to go back into the house. He closes the door and stands in front of it. "I think you two boys ought to move along right now. Okay?"

Pack Leader is shocked by the sudden rush of panic that goes through his stomach. He's also terrified that his cover might be blown. All Grinder can think about as he stares into the deputy's eyes is that bear up in Yellowstone that he tangled with. Both men offer their thanks and quickly get back to their van and drive off.

Jim pulls out a notebook from his pocket and writes down the description of the van, the men, and the license plate number. He can't help but notice how quickly that VW van accelerates. He looks down at the front end and notices that it raises slightly when the driver puts it into first, which shows there is quite a bit of torque being put on the driveline and U-joints. Also, the sound of the engine is all wrong for that model of van. Inside the house, Linda finally gets Thunder settled down.

Jim goes back in the house and tells Linda to not let anyone inside while he is not home. He then heads out to his squad car and grabs the radio that Joe Mason gave him to stay in contact with the highway patrol. He tells Joe that he's got to go down to Sheridan to check in with Al, then asks if they would keep an eye on Linda and Jacob as they patrol. Joe assures him that they will. Feeling a lot better, he gets in his patrol vehicle and goes to check in.

Inside the van, Pack Leader and Grinder both heave a sigh of relief to be away from the deputy. Grinder looks sideways at him while driving and says out of the corner of his mouth, "See what I mean? He looked like he wanted to kill both of us right there. That guy gives me the heebie-jeebies. Did you see that freaking wolf he's got?"

Pack Leader starts to play the whole scenario through his mind. "You know, when he answered the door, he didn't seem like anything special, but as soon as you kissed his wife's hand, he…like…*changed*!" He puts his hand to his chin and tries to run his fingers through his absent beard while thinking. "That's it! That's his trigger."

Grinder looks over. "What are you talking about?"

Pack Leader reaches over and slaps Grinder on the back of his head. "His family, stupid. Think about it. His wife and son are out there on the porch, and you walk up and grab and kiss her hand. You're a stranger to him. Remember what you said made him attack you last time? You threatened his wife."

Grinder leans back against the seat and sighs. "You're right. When he thinks his family is in danger, the bear comes out. Boss, we can't confront him around his wife and kid. He'll give us a war. If we touch them before he's dead, he'll never give up hunting us."

Pack Leader looks over at Grinder and rolls his eyes. "Yes, and you are the dumbass that had to go all Don Juan and kiss his wife's hand."

"I'm sorry, boss. You know how I get around a good-looking woman, and Deputy Dawg there has himself one fine piece of real estate."

Pack Leader tells him to head for the warehouse. "The only way we're going to kill that bastard without any collateral damage on our part is to bushwhack that son of a bitch. Catch him by surprise and take him down. I'll guarantee you whenever he's around those two, his radar is way too active. Nope, we'll have to lure him out, and take him out. We're also going to have to deal with those two highway patrol biker guys."

Grinder smiles and then howls the wolf cry. "And then I go and stake my claim to his little honey back there."

Chapter Nine
Everyone Wants to Hear This Story

Present Day, Rainbow Bar, Sheridan, Wyoming

Joe picks up his glass and finishes off the rest of his beer that has now gotten very warm. His nephew, Bill, is so intrigued by the story that he has sorely neglected his two customers. He looks up and shakes his head. "Sorry Joe, Marv. You guys want another drink?" They both say yes, and he turns around to get them refills.

When he returns, he notices a large, distinguished, athletic-looking African-American man with a slight touch of gray at his temples get up from a booth very close to where the three are sitting. The man came in about an hour and a half ago, ordered a beer and some nachos, and kept to himself.

The man walks over to Joe and sticks out his hand. "Major Joe Mason, I'm Captain Tommy Williams of the US Navy SEALs, retired. I couldn't help but hear the story you were telling about Jim Edwards and his family back in the early '70s. I know his son, Jacob, very well and have recently had the pleasure of meeting and spending some quality time with his father. Would you mind if I joined your little group?"

Joe stands up, shakes his hand, and offers him a seat. Meanwhile, Marv—who immediately recognizes the name and is now vibrating in his seat—waits while Tommy grabs his food and drink and joins them. As soon as Tommy puts his stuff on the bar, Marv jumps up and holds out his hand. "Captain Tommy Williams. Wow. The living legend, in the flesh. It's a pleasure to meet you, sir."

Tommy grabs the retired coast guardsman's hand and shakes it heartily. "I don't mind saying, Chief, that I hate it when people call me that. It makes me feel like I went and did something in my life that I have no recollection of."

Marv gives a sigh and a short whistle. "You mean like leading the rescue team that brought back the commander and his family?"

Tommy laughs and says, "Yeah, well, let's not forget that a good portion of that rescue team consisted of the commander's father and daughter. After what I saw those two accomplish, including the fact that they very nicely kept up with the four of us highly trained and skilled military people, the story I'm hearing from Joe here makes perfect sense."

Marv fills Joe and Bill in on who Captain Tommy Williams is and how he trained Jacob Edwards in a special program that taught SEAL tactics to other military and law enforcement agencies. Joe looks up at Tommy and smiles. "So, what brings you to our neck of the woods, Captain?"

Tommy holds out both hands to all three men. "To find out exactly what you three are talking about. You see, when we vetted then Lieutenant Jacob Edwards for our program, we ran into a huge roadblock looking up his dad's law enforcement record here in Sheridan. It was like someone had erased the last six months of his term as a deputy. And when I say erased, I am serious. All the written documents were blanked out. Someone did not want anyone to know what happened with Jim up there in Story. It almost cost Jacob his shot at the program, until I got this letter from a retired Marine Corps sergeant major here in Sheridan."

126

Tommy reaches inside his jacket and pulls out a yellowed piece of laminated paper with the Sheridan County Sheriff's Department heading on it. He then shows it to the trio.

Captain Williams,
If you and your black ops spook team keep trying to dig into Jim Edwards's past, I will have you up on charges for invasion of privacy and trying to strong-arm a law enforcement agency of Wyoming. Jim Edwards was the best damn deputy I ever trained. I've seen three wars and served my country for thirty years in the Marine Corps. There ain't a man alive I'd rather go into hell with to fight my way back out than him. I'll guarantee that if Little Chunk grew up to be half the man his old man is, then he's twice the man you ever had in your pansy outfit. Now, get off my back and stay out of Jim's business.

Lt. Al Freeburger
Sheridan County Sheriff's Department

"I showed this letter to the Secretary of the Navy when Al sent it back in '99. He took one look at it and said, 'If Sergeant Major Freeburger vouches for that family, then let the kid in the program and stop trying to dig up any more on his father.'"

Joe shakes his head and laughs. He asks Tommy to let him see it, looks it over for a few seconds, laughs again, and hands it back. "You know, there wasn't a cop or National Guardsman in the whole state of Wyoming who wasn't scared shitless of pissing Al off. When it came to Al's legendary connections, Sheriff Manning used to say that Al was his secret weapon. He was one hell of a guard dog at keeping state and federal assholes off the sheriff's back."

He looks over at Marv and wipes a tear out of his eye. "We sure miss that old scrapper of a grandpa you had." He raises his glass and says, "To Al Freeburger. What a lawman is supposed to be!" All four men raise their drinks in the air and say, "To Al." Tommy looks around and sees about a dozen older men in the bar raising their glasses as well.

Tommy puts his glass down and asks Bill why Jim left the sheriff's department in the first place. "From everything you said so far, it looked like Wyoming was going to have their own Dick Tracy. Then he just quit, moved to Alabama, and then to Pennsylvania to work with cars. Freeburger erased his last six months of logs and wouldn't talk to anyone but you about it. Why?"

Joe sits there for a minute, wondering how to proceed when all four men hear someone say from behind them, "Ah, hell, Joe. You might as well just tell him. It's the reason I brought him here in the first place. Past is past, and Al ain't around anymore to kick our asses for talking about it."

As the group turns around, they see Jim Edwards standing behind them. He looks over at Tommy and winks. "I thought if you hung out here long enough, someone would start talking about the lieutenant and the good old days."

Joe is immediately on his feet and walks over to embrace his old friend. "Damn, Jim. It's been a while. When was the last time you were home for a visit? It had to be before Cozumel happened. Believe it or not old buddy, Al ain't the subject of the conversation here. You are."

Before he can respond, Marv and Bill introduce themselves to Jim, and Marv tells him how he served under Jacob on the *First Responder* at Cozumel. The five of them decide that they are taking up way too much space at the bar, so Bill has a couple of tables pushed together so they can take seats around them. As the group settles in, the front door to the bar opens and another group of people walk in that has the five of them on their feet again. The new group consist of Linda, Jacob, Mary, Roberto, and Danielle Edwards; and Chris Rottanelli.

The six make their way to the other group. Marjorie gets another table and pushes it up to the two that are already together. Jacob looks over at Marv, gets a huge grin on his face, and grabs his hand. "Chief Schuette, is that you? Wow, you're back home. That's great!" Everyone in the party gets seated and orders refreshments. Little Roberto gets his first sip of a genuine western sarsaparilla soft drink. Introductions are made, then Marv asks why the whole family is in Sheridan so soon after the rescue. Linda tells him that they are heading down to South Texas for Marnia Gonzalez's wedding to Jonathan Carmichael next week, and Tommy begged them to detour up here first so that he could find out more about Jim serving with the famous Lieutenant Al Freeburger of the Sheridan County Sheriff's Department. Joe chuckles and tells everyone that he was telling Bill, Marv, and (inadvertently) Tommy the story of Jim's legendary stint with the sheriff's department.

Jim nervously clears his throat and asks how far they have gotten. Joe tells him that he just finished the part where Pack Leader and Grinder had the nerve to come to his door disguising themselves as tourists and inquiring about fishing.

Jim looks over at Joe and smiles. "I can take it from here, if you don't mind."

But all the other people sitting around the tables unanimously say no to that suggestion. Linda puts her hand on Jim's arm. "Please, darling, let Joe finish the story. All you'll try to do is downplay what you did. It's time that our family knows what really happened here and why we had to leave." She affectionately looks over at Joe and continues, "Besides, next to Al Freeburger, Joe is about the only other person I know who would tell it right. So go ahead, Joe."

Joe thanks Linda and then proceeds to catch the new people up on what has happened so far. To his delight, Jim's family has already been told bits and pieces of the story, with some big exceptions, like the time that Jim beat the hell out of Grinder for threatening Linda.

As Joe looks around, he notices for the first time that there is a whole crowd of other men and women standing around waiting for him to finish the story. So he looks at Jim and gets an ear-to-ear grin on his face. "You know, this ain't the first time that I've told this story. A bunch of us old-timer law dogs get together every once in a while up at a cabin off Red Grade and talk about 'The Legend of Deputy Jim.'"

Jim starts to jump out of his seat. "Oh, for crying out loud, Joe! Come on, no!"

But Linda pulls him down again and Joe continues the story.

Chapter Ten
Jim and Al Figure it Out

Sheridan County Sheriff's Department, Spring of 1974

Jim takes his time driving to work that morning. He is still upset over his encounter with the tourist guys in the souped-up VW van. He really cannot put his finger on why they bugged him so much. When that blond-haired guy grabbed and kissed Linda's hand, he felt like ripping both their heads off. He never considered himself the jealous type but those boys just bugged him the wrong way. The last thing he needed right now was to lose his temper over something stupid and have Al pissed off at him. He pulls into the department parking lot, gets out, takes a calming breath, and walks in to talk to Al about what just went down in Cheyenne.

Standing by the reception desk just inside the door are Al and Manning, talking about the news from Cheyenne. Manning says, "All four are dead. How is that even possible?"

Al shakes his head, takes off his hat, and rubs his eyes. "George, all I know is that Michaels called me up around four a.m. to tell me that Reno, Sisko, and Belinda were murdered last night, and we already know that Arson was found dead in his cell at the beginning of the week. They figured out that Arson was poisoned with some crap from South America called 'Angel's Breath.' It puts you in a state of amnesia, and if you take too much, it kills you while you sleep. Belinda and the other two had their necks broken. She was raped before she died."

Sheriff Manning closes his eyes, drops his chin to his chest, and shakes his head solemnly. He looks up to see Jim coming through the front door. "Al, you and Jim join me in my office in thirty minutes. I'm going to process this a while. Tell Lucy to hold all my calls until after we meet." He nods his head to Jim, then turns and walks to his office.

Jim starts to ask a question, but Al raises his hand to silence him. He motions Jim to the break room on the other side of the hall. They both walk in and find a table to sit at and talk. "So, you think it was a Medellin hitman that did all four, Lieutenant?"

Al leans in and says very quietly, "They arrested a big Mexican that night, supposedly from Texas, who managed to get himself in the security cell right next to Arson. Six hours later, Arson's dead. Four days later, the guy miraculously pays off his fine, leaves, and the rest are found dead the next day. You do the math, kid. Medellin just had all their tracks erased. They traced that Mexican to Phoenix and then he disappeared. He was supposed to go to Utah where he said he was contracted to pick melons. Hell, the only melon that guy ever picked was the one that sits between someone's ears."

As usual, Jim is writing everything down on his notepad. "You know, Lieutenant, those bikers showing up the way they did and then just disappearing has really got people spooked. Do we know anything?"

Al sits back in his chair, takes a long drag on his menthol cigarette and blows a couple of smoke rings in the air. "You remember the story of the Trojan Horse from Homer, kid?"

Jim looks up. "You mean how the Greeks hid inside that big horse they made and snuck into Troy so they could ransack the place? What about it?"

"Well, one thing you never expect a biker to be without is his bike. But what if somehow they snuck them into the area, kept them hidden, and only used them when they were out causing trouble?"

Jim sits back and thinks. "Okay, Al, that might be, but what about the bikers themselves? Hell, you can spot them a mile off. They all look like a bunch of wild wolves. It ain't like they could just check in to a motel somewhere and go unnoticed."

"You're right, but who said anything about using a motel? Look, most of these bikers are ex-military. Every kid I ever had in any unit was taught the same two things—how to hike and how to camp. This is the northwest, kid. We have the Rockies, Tetons, and the Bighorn Mountains all around us. You could be dropped off in Montana, Utah, or Idaho and basically hike your way in here and have a good chance of not being spotted. All you would have to do is hole up somewhere back up in the high country and come down every once in a while to do your business."

Jim sits straight up. "I get it, Lieutenant. Then you have your bikes snuck in on trucks and stowed someplace. You use regular cars, trucks, or vans to get to your bikes; then sneak out, do your thing, bring them back, and head back to your hiding place. So where are they hiding?"

Al stands up, puts his hat on, and winks. "Jim, that's the sixty-four-thousand-dollar question. And I know someone who can help us with that one. Right now, he's got his team up by Bear Lodge doing some surveying of park lands. After we meet with the sheriff, you're going to head up there and talk with Joe's dad, Ron Mason. He's been a park ranger around here going on thirty years, and he knows every trail leading into this valley from a 250-mile radius. I'm going up to the Billings hospital to talk to your cousins who were attacked by those bikers. They both got out of ICU yesterday and it looks like they'll make good recoveries.

I want to get to them before they're flown down to Denver for reconstructive surgery."

Jim was worried sick about his two cousins all week and went to his aunt and uncle's place several times to get updates. He knows that they are going to be okay and that the family has received a lot of help from the community to pay for the medical expenses. Their dad was also a pretty successful rancher northwest of Sheridan, so even the plastic surgery will be covered. As Jim and Al walk to Sheriff Manning's office, Jim thanks Al for the update.

George Manning wipes the tears from his eyes when he hears the knock on his door. He knows that Belinda was no good and deserved to go to jail for what she did, but he would never wish her fate on anyone, and especially on someone he thought he loved once. He straightens himself out, adjusts his clothing, and tells Al and Jim to come in. The trio talk about what Al and Jim discussed in the break room. Sheriff Manning likes the plan and approves. "Al, I got a telefax earlier today from the AG. The governor is probably going to mobilize the National Guard up here in Sheridan. When that happens, I lose you for a while. Make sure we're covered here when you're gone."

Al and Jim walk out of Sheriff Manning's office and head to their separate tasks. Al knows that George was probably in his office sulking about Belinda. George was one of the best officers he had ever served under in the marines. He was a major in Korea and the CO of Al's unit. Sheridan is damn lucky to have George as its sheriff. He knows how to run a good department and make sure everything works together just right. His record speaks for itself and he is one hell of a fine lawman, but when it comes to women, George is as stupid as a man can get. The prettier they are, the more gullible he is, and Belinda was a looker, all right. He knows George will pull it together and get on top of the business at hand.

Going the speed limit, Billings, Montana, is a two-hour drive from Sheridan straight north up Interstate I-90. Al makes it in ninety minutes. He walks into the lobby of the St. Vincent Hospital off 12th Street right at noon. The Beckers' parents are waiting for him there. The dad, who is also named Tim, walks up to Al and shakes his hand. "They will be flown down to Denver this afternoon. The doctor says that my son is willing to talk, but Megan is still way too shaken and won't talk to anyone but her mother and myself."

Al offers his condolences to Tim's wife, Sue, and they take him to Tim Jr.'s room.

As he walks into the private hospital room on the third floor, he sees two beds, one on each side of the room, but one is curtained off. He concludes that the curtained off one is Megan. He respects her privacy and walks straight over to Tim's bed. Tim's face and head are all bandaged up. His left eye and part of his jaw are covered. He turns to see his parents and Al enter the room. "Hello, Lieutenant Freeburger. I'm glad it's you that came up to talk. The only other one I would have wanted is my cousin Jim."

Al takes off his hat and sits next to Tim. "Well, I sent him up Dayton Kane Road to Bear Lodge to talk to Ron Mason at the Forest Service. I read the statements that your mom and dad sent us. Your dad here tells me you're ready to talk to me about what happened, so let me put this out here so it's official. Neither you nor your sister are in any trouble with the law. We know kids sneak up to the graveyard to party once in a while. After what you two went through, the sheriff, district attorney, Judge Reatle, and the mayor all agree that no charges will be filed against any of the kids who were attacked. For that matter, no one has said anything about why you kids were up there in the first place. We can't stop people from guessing, but no official word will be put out by any of us."

Tim's whole body visibly relaxes when Al finishes. There is a slight sigh that comes from behind the curtain and Sue disappears into it to check on her daughter. Al puts his hand on Tim's shoulder and asks him to tell him in his own words what happened. Tim takes a deep breath and tells Al the whole story, not leaving anything out. "When the biker, Grinder, attacked Megan, I really did everything I could to stop him, Lieutenant."

Al asks him if he is sure it was Grinder. "I accused him of being Grinder, and he didn't deny it. He made some excuse about Jim catching him off guard. After Megan clocked him on the head, he went berserk. I didn't think I could get up and fight after being racked by that jerk. But I did get up and managed to give him a good fight before I went down. I guess I'm just not as tough as Jim."

Al puts his hand on the boy's shoulder and shakes it. "Son, who the hell knows what would have happened if Grinder had gotten up after Jim beat him down those steps. Hell, Tim, there were at least a dozen peace officers there, and I had my .357 aimed right at his forehead. I guess we'll never know. If it's any consolation, you and Jim are the only two people I have ever heard of who stood up to Grinder like that. Of that alone, you should be proud."

Tim's dad stands a little straighter and his son grins so big that his face hurts from the effort. "Well, I did rip half his beard off when he threw me down for the last time. Funny thing is, I don't think he screamed or nothing when I did. You'd think something like that would really hurt."

"That's because his beard and mustache were fake. When he came over and crawled on top of me, I started to scream and pull at the rest of his beard. It was glued on and came off pretty easily."

The three men look over at the curtain as Tim's mom, Sue, starts to open it. She gets halfway and then hesitates. "Go ahead, Mom. It's okay. I want to talk now."

They see Megan lying on her bed with her face and head bandaged up. She props herself up on her elbows and looks at the group. "When I did that, he got so mad that he grabbed and ripped out half my hair. The doctors here don't know if it will grow back. That's one of the reasons why we're going to Denver. Mom found a specialist down there who might be able to help me with...what's that procedure called, Mom?"

"Follicle regrowth and transplant surgery."

Tim adds, "I just need some bridge work and to have my jaw wired for a while. They say someday, if I want, they can take away the scars. But I didn't want to leave Megan alone, so we're going to have all those surgeries in Denver at the same hospital."

Al can't help but be moved by these two brave kids. In his over forty years of military and law enforcement, he's seen a lot of good kids go through even worse, but something about the way this brother tried to stand up for his sister really gets to him. Despite himself, he takes his hand and clears a tear from his eye. He takes out his notepad and writes all this new info down. "You know, bikers don't shave or cut their hair for no one no how. For the ex-military ones, it's their way of giving the middle finger to Uncle Sam. If Grinder doesn't have a beard or long hair, then it's the first time since he was dishonorably discharged and got out of jail. So he either got into some kind of freak accident, or he and his buddies are pulling some kind of ruse and maybe even hiding in plain sight. No one would ever recognize any of those boys clean-cut and shaven."

He looks up from his pad and realizes he had been thinking out loud. "Well, folks, that's just me trying to sort things out. I think we have enough from these two youngsters to get us a step closer to nailing these creeps." He then looks over at the Beckers and says, "You keep these two away from Sheridan until this is done. Grinder and his boss, Pack Leader, are vindictive sons of bitches and won't hesitate to go after them if they can."

Megan sits straight up in her bed and says, "Lieutenant Freeburger, I only ask one thing."

"What's that, honey?"

"Stop those bastards and make sure they can never do this to anybody again."

Al puts his hat back on his head, stands up, and starts to walk out of the room. He turns and says, "Megan, I'll make that happen or die trying."

Al leaves the hospital with a couple of really good ideas, and the first one he can take care of right there in Billings. He heads over to the local sheriff's office and manages to catch his counterpart, Bill Roberts.

Bill has been with the Billings sheriff's department for about eight years, and Al likes him because like himself, Bill was a marine. He is a retired gunny who spent a lot of time in Nam and a few more years training recruits. He is tough, salty, and knows how the real world works—Al's kind of people. He walks into the main office and sees Bill walking down the hall with a sandwich in his hand, hurrying off somewhere. "Well, I'll be a son of a bitch. I didn't know that a gunny could walk and eat at the same time."

Bill looks up and gets a huge grin on his face. "Back in Nam, Sergeant Major Freeburger never let any of us sit long enough to eat, so we all had to learn to improvise. How you doing, Al?"

Al laughs, walks up, and slaps Bill on the back. "I'm okay. I need to borrow your telefax. I want to get some records transferred to Sheridan from marine and army HQs. The sooner I send the requests, the sooner they can overnight mail them to me."

Bill looks at Al and chuckles. "So, when do you want those files? Next month? You and I both know that if you send a telefax it'll go through fifty channels before it's even considered."

Bill takes what's left of his sandwich, shoves it in his mouth and motions for Al to follow him. They go straight to the vacated office of the Billings sheriff, who is out of town for a couple of days. When they get in, he points to the seat behind the desk. "The phone is to your right. Use line one; you can call anyone anywhere on that one. I got to go and arrest a bank manager who's embezzling funds. Just write down where you called and why. I'll square it with the sheriff when he gets back. He'll love having a reason to call Manning and yell at him about something. It'll give both of them an excuse to talk about their next fishing trip."

Al sits down at the Billings sheriff's desk and makes a bunch of phone calls to the Pentagon, Marine Corps, and army HQ in DC. He finally ends up having a lengthy conversation with a two-star Marine Corps general he served with in World War II. When he's done, he has a guarantee that he will have all the files he wants flown into the Sheridan airport by tomorrow afternoon. He thanks the general, hangs up, and walks out to the receptionist's desk and hands her an envelope with Lieutenant Roberts's name on it. In it is a detailed list of the phone calls he made and why.

When he gets back in his squad car, he thinks that he is not in such a hurry to get back, so he grabs a bite to eat at a burger joint. He then finds Bill Roberts and catches up a little, and then drives the speed limit back to Sheridan. He rolls into town around 10:00 p.m. In hindsight, he wishes that he had just hightailed it back as soon as possible.

Earlier That Day, Ranger Station Up Near Bear Lodge

Jim knows this area pretty well because his dad bought a cabin up here a few years ago, and once in a while he'd grab Linda, Jacob, and Thunder and go up there for a weekend. The ranger station is just five miles north of Bear Lodge and a little bit closer to the cabin. Jim pulls up and gets out to walk up the hill, where the station sits on elevated stilts. He has already radioed ahead to make sure that Ranger Mason is there. He climbs the wooden steps, knocks on the door and an older version of Joe Mason greets him. Ron Mason invites him in.

Jim shakes the senior ranger's hand. "Thanks for meeting with me today. I know you guys have your hands full with all the surveying going on, but Lieutenant Freeburger wanted me to ask you a few questions about some trails that lead into the Sheridan Valley from other states. He seems to think that a group of men could start out in Montana or Idaho and hike in here pretty much undetected. Is that true?"

Ron walks over to a topographical map on a table at the far end of the room. It displays the whole of the Rocky Mountain range, from Mexico into Canada. Both men stand and stare at the map for a while. Ron is just past sixty years old, clean-shaven, large, and muscular like his son, and has the weather-burned face of a man that has spent most of his life outdoors. He puts his hand to his chin and walks around back to look at the map from the Canadian end going down through the United States. He points at the Continental Divide first. "We've known for a long time that there are a whole bunch of people who basically live hiking up and down the Divide. They're pretty much what's left of the old mountain man culture. Some of them don't even have birth certificates or social security numbers. They were born and raised up there."

He looks up and smiles at Jim. "You may not remember this because it happened when you were just a kid, but one of these guys had three sons back then and none of them had any wives. So they all waited for the right car to pull off at a rest stop in the Colorado Rockies on 70. They were college girls headed to Las

Vegas. The dad and his boys jumped them and kidnapped them. It took us over two years to track them down up there. By the time we caught up with that family, two of the girls had already had babies and did not want to leave their babies' daddies. If it weren't for the third one being willing to press charges, we would not have even had a case, because all the girls were over twenty-one when the mountain men took them.

"Now the FBI is telling us that they believe some of these mountain men are helping South American cartels smuggle drugs into the US, so there's a lot more attention on these guys now, but no real arrests have been made yet because these boys are good at hiding. Except for Interstates 70, 80, and 90 that cross the Rockies, there are not many places where these people can be exposed. They are better woodsmen than most of my rangers and pretty much live undetected."

Ron shakes his head and rubs his chin again as he ponders the map. "But the Divide can't get you undetected into Sheridan Valley, and I don't believe a group of hikers can get into the Sheridan Valley undetected very easily from Idaho or Utah." He takes his finger and points it to a region in Montana that is just north of Sheridan and runs it along a trail that ends just north of Story. The path is a 125-mile hike from Fort Smith, Montana, to Story, Wyoming, down the Bighorn Mountain range. He looks up at Jim and smiles. "If I wanted to sneak into Sheridan County undetected, this is the trail I'd take. It's about a two-to-three-week hike, depending on how fast you travel and how good you are at hiking."

It bothers Jim when he hears about the bikers possibly coming into the area right where he lives. He leans down and looks at the detail of the topography in the trail Ron is referring to and points out that there are several streams that a hiker would have to cross. Ron tells him that they are not that deep and can be crossed on the trail and would make it easier for hikers to hydrate and maintain a semblance of trail hygiene. Jim thanks Ron for the information and is about to leave, but Ron invites him over to Bear Lodge for some lunch. Jim never turns down a free meal, especially one that involves a steak cooked on the mountain, so Ron closes up the station and they head over.

Bear Lodge is a quick, ten-minute drive from the ranger station and is known for its rustic atmosphere and succulent, charbroiled hamburgers and steaks. As they are finishing their meal, Ron asks how his son, Joe, is doing in the "Motorcycle Brigade," as he liked to call it. Jim tells him that outside of the freak attack at Little Goose Canyon a week ago, biker-related crime in his territory has been next to nothing since Joe and his partner started patrolling there. Ron sits back, wipes his mouth with a napkin, and with obvious fatherly pride says, "Well, there is only one thing my boy loves more than football, and that's riding a bike."

Jim laughs. "Yes, and when I found out his partner was Jerry Gibes, the Natrona County quarterback who led his team to the state championship over Joe and our boys, I about fell off my seat laughing my head off." Ron gets an ear-to-ear grin and says that it's still the biggest family joke on him at the supper table whenever he comes home for a visit. The two get up and get ready to head to the register when they hear some arguing coming from that direction.

A tall, thin man, slightly balding on top is red-faced and arguing with two teenage boys. "I'm telling you that you and your friend cannot come in here like that. You two boys need to go get cleaned up. Now get out. You're stinking the place up."

Jim and Ron round the corner and see that the manager of Bear Lodge is arguing with some very scruffy-looking young men who look like they have been out in the woods for weeks. When they get a little closer, Jim can smell them. Ron pulls out a hand-kerchief and Jim just covers his nose. The manager looks up and sees Jim coming over. He walks out from behind the cash register and flails his arms. "Deputy, thank God. I was just about ready to send for you. These two boys are from Sheridan and they just got back from a ten-day hike and want me to serve them in our restaurant!"

Jim looks around the lodge and notices that a lot of the patrons are starting to hold their noses and wave their hands in front of their faces. He turns back to the boys with a half grin, half smirk. "Okay, guys, let's continue this conversation outside before we have a riot on our hands."

Once outside, the smaller of the two hikers starts waving his arms and yelling. "You can't refuse us service just because we haven't had a bath yet! Man, we just got off the mountain trail and we're both starving. This ain't right."

Before Jim can say a thing, Ron steps forward and tells the manager to get the boys a couple of hamburgers and bring them out here. He laughs, winks at Jim, and turns his attention to the boys. "You two just came off the north trail up behind the lodge here, didn't you?" They both nod. Ron continues, "I am guessing neither one of you were in the Boy Scouts or had dads who taught you how to camp, huh?"

The two start to settle down and look at the ground, kicking the dirt like they are embarrassed. "No, but I checked out a book from the library and we did everything it said about navigating the trail and marking our progress. Plus, we learned how to read the map really good. We never got lost once, and you didn't have to come up and save us or anything. We also planned our meals really good too. We ate the last meal this morning and hiked in here expecting to get supper before my mom picks us up in a couple of hours."

By now, Jim and Ron have placed themselves upwind of the two boys so they could breathe a little easier. Ron continues, "Tell me, son, was there a section in that book of yours on camping and hiking hygiene?"

"Well, yes, but I didn't read that part because I figured it wasn't part of survival. And we did this to learn survival."

Jim and Ron start laughing. "Well, after ten days out there in the mountains, didn't you think to clean up or change your clothes?" Jim asks.

The boys both shake their heads and Ron looks down at the ground and gives a big whistle. "Boys, you might have survived ten days up there okay, but if someone has to be around you for very long in a car going down the mountain, I don't give them a snowball's chance in hell of surviving. What's your poor mom supposed to do when she picks you up? Strap you to the roof and carry you down like that?"

Ron tells the boys that he's got some extra clothes up at the station and some garbage bags for their old ones. "You can use the outdoor shower up there to clean up before your mom gets here." He then tells them to crawl in the back of the ranger truck and he'll take them up in a moment. By this time, the manager brings out the hamburger meals which the two wolf down almost instantly and then get in the back of the truck.

Jim looks at the old ranger and asks, "So, after the shower and change of clothes, are they going to be okay riding down with the boy's mom?"

Ron chuckles. "Well, they'll be a hell of a lot better, but it's going to take a couple of good cleans to really beat all that smell out of them. If they had practiced some basic hygiene up there, one good shower would have done it."

At that, Ron shakes Jim's hand and Jim thanks him for all the information. Ron tells him to bring his family and come by with

Joe someday for a good chicken dinner. Jim just says, "You don't have to ask me that one twice," and then gets in his squad car and leaves. By the time he gets back to Sheridan, he wishes he had left the two rank hikers for Ron to deal with alone.

Chapter Eleven
Bikers Don't Know When to Quit

9:00 p.m., Kendrick Park, Sheridan, Wyoming

Pack Leader figures that a week is a long enough break to keep Sheridan on edge but not lull them to sleep about the "ghost bikers" attacking again. This time, he uses the old moving-van panel trucks provided by his friends down south to bring his and his buddies' choppers up to the fairgrounds on 5th Street. Those old, white trucks were seen all over town doing things like moving furniture and transporting produce and other things, so they were pretty much ignored.

Once they unload the bikes out behind the roller rink building, he and Grinder and the five others with them put on their biker clothes, wigs, and fake beards. Grinder has to settle for a light brown hair and beard color because that little bitch and her brother that he attacked last time ruined his blond set. Once they are all set up, they take out some retrofitted muffler inserts that they attached to the ends of the very loud Harley mufflers to quiet the bikes down, and then they ride over to Kendrick Park. The park closes at 8:00 p.m., but Pack Leader knows that he can find some kids partying in a special spot.

Back in the '60s, someone had the big idea to put a little zoo area right up against the hill in the park. They had some special kennels and cages built to house different animals indigenous to the area. One cage was for housing a couple of big brown bears. The cage had a manmade cave built in the back of it for the bears to sleep in. A couple of years ago, the mayor at the time felt that it was not in the city's best financial interest to support the animals, so they were transferred to another zoo and all the bars were taken down from the cages.

Someone should have figured out then that something like a bunch of open cages with deep, dark caves built in the back would spell nothing but trouble when it came to curious teenagers, especially the ones looking for a cool place to party. The seven bikers quietly ride over to the high school that sits on a hill just above the park. Pack Leader makes them all shut down their bikes and walk down a very steep road that leads into the park. The road runs directly over the old zoo area.

Meanwhile, Grinder has left his bike and scaled the hill to check if anyone is in the caves.

Meanwhile, inside the bear cave in the park, Tony is really excited that Beth had invited Julia to come and smoke some weed with them in the bear caves that night. She is new to Sheridan and he had been trying to get to know her all winter after she transferred from Laramie in January. She is smoking hot and lights up the halls of his school every time he sees her. His best friend, Sam, is also there with his longtime girlfriend, Tina. Even though Beth is cute, Tony just never was that into her, outside of being friends. She obviously had a crush on him and would basically do anything to please him, even if that meant inviting another girl along that she knows he likes.

He had brought a quarter-pound of some good, homegrown stuff. Sam brought his bong and they were already passing it around for the second time. Tony is feeling the courage of the toke taking hold, and he gets up and starts to walk over to where Julia is sitting next to Beth when all five kids freeze in fear at the sound of a voice coming from the mouth of the cave.

"You kids are going to want to come out here so that we can all have a nice party, okay?"

Tony kind of sinks down to his seat, but Sam has never been one to be pushed around. He gets on his feet and goes to the mouth of the cave. "Look, asshole, we were here first. So, if you don't want your face caved in, I suggest you leave." With that, Grinder reaches in and grabs the kid, cuffing his hand around the back of his neck, and yanks him out into the middle of the pen and slams him down on the concrete.

By this time, five of the six bikers are down by the cage on their choppers, and Grinder runs back up to get his. The other biker is over by the outdoor amphitheater at the entrance to the park looking for Sheridan PD patrols. They were told that the locals start patrolling the park every twenty minutes after midnight, but just sporadically before that.

Pack Leader gets off his bike and walks over to the cave mouth. "If I don't see some asses out here in about two seconds, I'll splat this little idiot's brain all over the concrete." He takes a deep inhale with his nose and continues, "That smells like some pretty good shit you got in there. Bring it and the bong out with you."

Within a minute, three crying girls and one petrified boy are standing behind their unconscious friend lying on the pavement. To Pack Leader's and Grinder's disgust, the boy is crying and carrying on, more frantic and terrified than the three girls. To their delight, all three girls are pretty good-looking with nice enough figures to be interesting.

Pack Leader knows that he has to keep a tight leash on his Wolf pack, because he wants to get as much impact out of this situation as he can. He and Grinder had already discussed that, like before, they needed to leave some alive so that they can tell the horror story. He quickly decides that since the one on the concrete had enough balls to try to stand up to Grinder, he's going to live.

Then he notices one of the girls trying to comfort the other boy, who looks about ready to soil his pants. Pack Leader has always prided himself on being able to size up people pretty fast. He decides that if she is more worried about someone else than herself, she will sing this story for the rest of her life with unbreakable passion. That was just the kind of PR he was looking for. He looks over at Grinder. "That one is yours. Take her back in the cave and make sure she's breathing when you're done." Grinder smiles from ear to ear, grabs the girl named Beth, and heads back into the cave.

Pack Leader then looks back at the remaining four bikers. Two of them were with him at the canyon last week and got to have some fun with the girls there. The other two were with Grinder and had chased down and killed the two greasers in the graveyard. He tells the second two that they can have the other two girls. He then grabs the boy, yanks him off the ground where he was groveling and tells the last of the bikers to follow him. He walks the kid over across the park to the foot bridge that goes over Little Goose Creek.

As soon as the bikers are all done with the night's activities, Pack Leader has them take their muffler inserts off their bikes, start them up, and take a lap around the park, howling and revving their engines. It does not take long for people who live close by to call the police. When they are done making noise, he tells them to put the inserts back on. But one of the Wolves out of the seven keeps his muffler open, heads out of the park, and takes the road out of town that leads toward the golf course. Three cop cars follow him while one sheriff's car goes in to investigate the park. Pack Leader, Grinder, and the four remaining bikers push their choppers back up the steep hill to the high school and take their muffled choppers back to the fairgrounds where they put them back in the panel trucks and head back to Story.

When the authorities arrive, Tony is lying in the middle of the creek with his neck broken; and Julia and Tina are lying on the bear cage floor, ravaged and dead. Beth is inside the bear cave, ravaged and beaten but still alive. Sam opens his eyes and finds himself seated in a corner with his hands and feet tied together, and with one sock stuffed in his mouth and another tied around his neck, holding it in place. He hears loud police sirens and the sound of a Harley Davidson chopper racing away.

The seventh biker's chopper is found abandoned on a dirt road north of town that goes straight into Dayton. The chopper is later ID'd as one with Wild Wolves markings on it. A little later that night, the biker goes to the little park in Dayton, where he finds a duffel bag with some clothes in it. He takes off his fake beard, wig, and Wild Wolves biker clothes and burns them in a barbeque pit there.

About 3:30 that morning, a clean-cut young man in Levi's, a T-shirt, and white sneakers walks up to a sky-blue 1969 Toyota Corona 4-speed. As he is getting in, a Sheridan County deputy stops him and searches him and his car. He tells the deputy that he was with some friends up at Arrowhead Lodge earlier and they just dropped him off. Fortunately for him, he is still a pledge member of the Wild Wolves and has not earned his Wolf tattoo yet. The deputy does not yet know what Al had figured out about how they are hiding in plain sight, so he lets the biker go. He gets in the car and drives up to Sheridan for some breakfast at the port of entry truck stop off I-90 and then heads to Story around 7:00 a.m.

Earlier That Evening

Al and Jim return to Sheridan at the same time that evening. As they are pulling up to the sheriff's department behind the court-house, they hear the call on their radios. Al sticks his head out the window of his cruiser and hollers for Jim to get in with him. Jim jumps in and Al turns on his siren and lights and heads right for the park. Al has a pretty good idea where to check first when they get there. He drives right over to the old zoo area and parks in front of the bear cage.

Jim had only been on the force for a little over two years, and what is on that floor next to the bear cave is by far the worst thing he has ever seen. Al sees that the kid is shocked out of his mind by the two dead teenage girls in front of him and tells Jim to go help the boy who is tied up in the corner. When he gets the sock out of Sam's mouth, the boy yells, "Beth is in the cave! I think I heard her moan a little while ago. She might be alive."

Jim gets the boy's hands and feet free and rushes into the cave with his flashlight and pistol drawn. Sam gets up and goes over to the girls' dead bodies. "Oh my God. Tina. Look what they did to her!" He falls on her body and for the first time that night he starts to cry uncontrollably. Al hates to do it, but he has to pull the boy off his dead girlfriend because he doesn't want any evidence messed up.

From inside the cave he hears Jim's voice. "Lieutenant, she's alive but pretty beaten up. We are going to need an ambulance." Later, a Sheridan PD officer finds the body of Tony in the creek below the footbridge.

Jim tells Al that he learned some interesting things up on the mountain while talking to Ranger Chief Ron Mason. Al tells him that he's got some stuff figured out as well. "Best thing the both of us can do now, kid, is get some shut-eye. Manning and the police chief can handle stuff for a while. I am beat. Go home."

By the time the crime scene is being wrapped up and the coroner is allowed to take the bodies, it is almost 6:00 a.m. The whole park gets sealed off for the next two days and Sheridan County is in a literal state of panic.

Chapter Twelve
Sheridan County
Biker Offensive

Later That Afternoon, Office of John Stalker,
Wyoming Attorney General

John has taken a good look lately at who his real friends are, and right at the top of the list are Sheriff George Manning and Lieutenant Al Freeburger of the Sheridan County Sheriff's Department. He also has grown quite fond of—and very interested in—their new deputy, Jim Edwards. One thing he doesn't want to see is any one of them getting hurt, and this last attack in Sheridan has got his boss, the governor, very worried.

He reaches over and picks up his phone to call the Wyoming National Guard Headquarters in Cheyenne. "Yes, this is Attorney General John Stalker. Connect me to Colonel Anderson's private line, please."

A familiar voice answers the phone and with a chuckle says, "Finally going to take me up on my offer and enlist for all those extra benefits, John?"

John chuckles because he knows that one of Tom's biggest headaches is keeping enough people in the Guard to qualify for a good budget every year. "Yes, that will happen the day you decide to go back to school and get a law degree, so you can help me out.

Okay, buddy?" Both men laugh at the old joke. John continues, "Anyway, Colonel, the governor is getting pretty worried about what is going on up in Sheridan. There was another attack last night by 'the ghost bikers,' and he's talking about activating the Guard up there."

The colonel sits back in his chair and sighs. "John, all three of my officers up there are out. One is on a special assignment for his other government job in DC and the other two are out of the country."

John rolls his eyes and responds. "Good gawd, Tom. You know those three could not handle something like this, anyway. Two of them never saw combat, and the other one did only one tour in Nam as a private. Then he came back and went to college and only did the Guard to help him pay for his law degree. Besides, you have Al Freeburger up there, and he's the highest-ranking NCO in the state and probably the most competent soldier and lawman we have. He never listens to those guys, anyway."

Tom rolls his eyes. "Yes, I know. I'm the only full bird in the state and he barely listens to me. That old ground-pounding mud-eater can handle anything you want to throw at him. But what's Manning going to say when we pull him? I'm sure he's about to lose his mind with that shit storm biker crisis."

John laughs. "Hell, Tom, if the governor activates a hundred Guardsmen, and you put Freeburger in charge, Manning's going to want to buy you a steak dinner at the Sheridan Inn next time you're up here. He'll be doing cartwheels for all the extra help."

Colonel Anderson tells the AG that he will be ready when the governor calls. He decides that a little bit of preparation won't hurt, so he gets on the phone with his quartermaster and arranges to have a convoy of extra men and equipment transferred to Sheridan that afternoon.

Next Day, Wild Wolves Winter Camp, Arizona

Renaldo Manerez never likes being an errand boy, but Señor Escobar did not want anyone else but him to handle this. So he uses his contacts at the border patrol in Arizona and has himself and his son, Maximillian, snuck in so they could set things up with the Wild Wolves. Their contacts in Wyoming say they spotted a National Guard convoy pulling into Sheridan the previous evening. It's now time to escalate the biker crisis in Sheridan and provide cover for moving all of their operations to the new location in Colorado. He gets out of the border patrol Jeep that belongs to a certain sergeant who has been on their payroll for a while. He and Maximillian take a look around to size up the situation.

They contacted one of Pack Leader's lieutenants yesterday, but he was nowhere to be seen. But just before he gets too irritated and starts yelling at people, he hears the voice of the man he's looking for.

"Right on time, Renaldo. To tell you the truth, I didn't know if you were serious or not." The duo turns around to see a very large, muscular, Mexican-American man standing behind them named Alfonso Torres—or "Demolisher," as he's known among the bikers—next to Pack Leader and Grinder. He is the toughest Wolf in the pack, and he also has an affinity for blowing things up whenever he gets the chance.

Renaldo smiles from ear to ear. "Alfonso, we would never abandon the Wolves. You have been some of our best business associates for far too long. Señor Escobar wants your gang to know we take care of our own." He looks over his shoulder and tells the border patrol sergeant to leave and come back in an hour.

As the man leaves, Renaldo looks at his son and says, "When you have the police in your pocket, especially on this side of the border, the less they know about your business, the better.

Because when they get caught by their superiors, and they almost always do, then they have less they can rat out on you."

Maximillian looks over at the sergeant as he drives away. "If he is stupid enough to rat you out, Father, then he will soon find it very hard to breathe with all the bullets I will put in his lungs."

Demolisher listens to the exchange between father and son and shakes his head and laughs. "Maximillian, I heard you were a firecracker growing into some kick-ass TNT. Guess the rumors are true. So how is the Medellin Cartel supposed to help us get Pack Leader, Grinder, and our boys back? I just heard the National Guard got activated in Wyoming and they're on the lookout for bikers at every border crossing."

As Demolisher is speaking, ten eighteen-wheeler big rig diesel trucks pull up to the camp. Renaldo smiles again and takes a big drag from his cigar. "Because, my friend, you and your gang and all of your bikes will be hidden in these when you cross the border into Wyoming. They are going to take your whole gang up and drop you off just north of Sheridan near Buffalo right where I-25 and I-90 meet. There you will wait until they drive past Sheridan into Montana. We've paid off the Indian Reservation police to hide them there until you can meet up with your friends. Then you will once again hide in the trucks, and they will do a whole route through Montana, Idaho, Utah, and on down to this place here in Arizona, where you all can be home free."

Demolisher is stunned by the brilliance of the plan. Everyone knows that bikers and truckers hate each other. No highway cop would ever suspect a bunch of truckers smuggling them in and out of an area. He has to admit, Pack Leader himself could not have come up with a better scheme. "So when are we going to get this little party started? Pack Leader called yesterday and said that once they take out the deputy and those two motorcycle cops, they are leaving, one way or another."

Renaldo subtly smiles. He knows that Pack Leader will probably bail on him before he gives the word to leave, but it's better to let him think he's in control so he doesn't figure out that his cartel associates already know everything and have plans of their own. "Have your gang ready to leave tomorrow morning. We have room for one hundred men and their bikes. We have also brought you some extra firepower."

By this time, the men are over behind one of the trucks and Maximillian opens the door to the back. When it's opened, Demolisher's heart goes into his throat. In it are several crates packed with semiautomatic assault rifles and Korean War-era grenades. He lets out a big whistle, looks back at Renaldo, and winks.

"You'll also find mounts and holsters in there that will allow your men to carry that equipment on your bikes," Renaldo says as he returns the wink. Renaldo finishes the conversation by telling Demolisher that once they have Pack Leader and Grinder safe, they are to report to the new cartel safe house over on Falcon Lake, just across the border from Texas. There, they can collect the rest of the money he promised them.

The border patrol sergeant who dropped off Renaldo and his son then pulls up to collect the two cartel men to sneak them back across the border. By the next morning, a hundred Wild Wolves and their bikes are riding in the back of ten eighteen-wheelers headed north on I-25 toward Wyoming.

Next Day around Noon, Conference Room, Sheriff's Department, Sheridan, Wyoming

For the last two days, it has been pure pandemonium around the whole county. The mayor has issued an 8:00 p.m. curfew for anyone under the age of twenty-one, and no one is allowed on the streets anywhere in the county after midnight. Al and Jim had a chance to talk over what they learned when they both went intel-gathering the other day. Plus, Jim followed the path of the biker who got away from the Sheridan PD and found the fire pit where he burned his clothes. Near that path he also found a retrofitted attachment that he later figured out was made specifically for a Harley Davidson chopper muffler. He told Al that if they put this on their choppers, it would significantly silence the noise that Harleys are so famous for. The abandoned chopper did not have a license plate or any other identifying paraphernalia, save for the Wild Wolves emblem on the gas tank. The muffler insert fit perfectly on the tail pipe.

Al got his package from Marine Corps HQ as promised and has its contents in his hand for the meeting he is participating in. Seated in front of George Manning and Sheridan Police Chief Charlie Jones are highway patrolmen Joe Mason and Jerry Gibes; Lieutenant Al Freeburger, who just happens to be in his National Guard Sergeant Major's uniform; AG chief investigator Donald Michaels; and Deputy Jim Edwards. The sheriff and the police chief look like they have not slept in a week. For that matter, neither has anyone else.

George clears his throat and begins. "Here's what we know. The Wolves snuck in here without their bikes a while back. It looks like they had them transported in on food trucks and vans all winter long. From what Al and Jim have pieced together, it would appear that they hiked down a trail from Montana that leads out just above Story. Jim here thinks they maintained a military-style hygiene discipline while on the trail to ensure that no one flagged them as deep-woods backpackers, and Al has confirmed this by adding that they must have shaved and cleaned up so they would be unrecognizable to most people."

Some of the men in the room give an exasperated sigh, but George holds up his hand in a calming gesture. "It's not as bad as you think. Now, Al here has been called into duty with the National Guard and has to report in about twenty minutes, so I'll let him take it from here."

Al stands up and pulls out some manila envelopes from his satchel containing photocopied pictures and hands each man in the room one envelope. "I asked a two-star Marine Corps general friend of mine at the Pentagon to rush these to me the other day. These are military discharge photos of Pack Leader, Grinder, and twenty of their top riders in the Wild Wolves. As you can see, they are all clean-shaven and have their grunt haircuts on. It should be a lot easier to ID any of these assholes now."

The police chief raises his hand. "Al, every eyewitness victim that we have talked to says the men who attacked them looked and dressed like bikers."

Al looks down at his watch and then at Manning, who just nods his head. "Folks, the governor called my unit up this morning and just reinforced us with supplies and men yesterday. I have been given command of the Sheridan County biker offensive and I've got to go now. So I'm going to let Jim here fill you in on the rest of the details."

The police chief looks a little perturbed as Al exits the room and Jim steps over by the sheriff. Manning chuckles. "Charlie, this kid can hold his own. Give him a chance."

Jim takes a big gulp and begins. "When I followed the tracks of the biker that we lost on his way to Ranchester, I came across a warm fire pit in the town park. When I examined it closely, I found that there were Levi's brass buttons and a zipper in there, which told me that he disrobed, burned his old clothes, and changed into some others, probably something inconspicuous.

Also, on the edge of the pit I found some partially burned hair. We sent that on to a lab down in Casper and they called us this morning to confirm that it's animal hair that had traces of glue on one end which showed it was part of a wig or beard. So the lieutenant and I have concluded that the Wolves are using these wigs and beards along with their biker clothes when they go out to attack the kids. Then, when they're done, they go back to wherever it is they are hiding and change into their clean-shaven personas, hide their bikes, and blend in. Now that it's May, we have enough tourists coming in that new faces won't catch anyone's attention."

He holds up the Harley muffler insert. "As most of you know, the bikers are using these to quietly get from one place to another undetected. We tested this one out on the bike we confiscated the other day and it makes them quieter than a four-cylinder Toyota car, but it also cuts the power by half. That's probably why I found this one. The biker had to take it off when he was being chased, loosely shoved it in his clothing somehow, and lost it on the trail when he took off on foot. They might not even know that we have this."

Donald Michaels of the attorney general's office raises his hand and stands up. "Can I look at that again, Jim?"

Jim nods and hands the piece to him. Michaels turns it over in his hands, studies it for a moment, and hands it back to Jim. "No one made that baby overnight. It's very good, machined equipment that probably cost a fortune to make. My guess is that they were somehow made south of the border and brought up to the Wild Wolves to use. One thing the AG and I agree on is that what's going on up here in Sheridan is a lot more complicated than a bunch of bikers losing their minds and going on a rape and murder spree. Sheriff Manning, Al, and Jim have already shut down one meth lab up on Casper Mountain and caused another up in Cody to pack up and leave. It doesn't make any sense that these bikers up here are trying to operate a major meth lab and then bring our attention on them like they have.

"What we have here is a distraction. First, it was intended to keep our attention off Casper and Cody, but thanks to Sheriff Manning, Al, and your junior Dick Tracy over there," motioning to Jim with his chin, "that is history, but someone still wants us totally focused on Sheridan. I believe that someone is Renaldo Manerez of the Medellin Cartel. They are moving their operations here in the northwest and this is just a distraction to keep us from figuring out where. Because of the four murders—or better yet, assassinations—that happened last week, we also believe that Pack Leader and Grinder are only partially aware of what the Medellins are doing. Renaldo, in my opinion, is banking on us finding and killing most of the Wolves to cover his trail. But Pack Leader, aka Captain Seth Brown, is no dummy. He was special ops Marine Corps recon in Nam back in '65 and one of the smartest combat field strategists we had. My bet is that he is a lot more aware of what his cartel friends are doing than they want him to be."

Manning interjects. "So what exactly are you saying, Donald? With Al in command of over one hundred guardsmen, if he's met with resistance, there's going to be a bloodbath, and we know all the force recon special op characters in bikerdom won't stand a chance against that salty old warhorse. With what the governor sent him yesterday, he'll turn them into vulture food."

Michaels smiles. "No one knows that better than you and I do, Sheriff. But I did talk to Al earlier, and we both agree that taking prisoner as many Wolves as we can is paramount. He believes they are going to show up on I-90 past Buffalo sometime this evening. And as you probably can guess, he's going to have one hell of a surprise for them when they head toward town."

The sheriff thanks everyone for their time and dismisses the group. While heading out, Jim comes up to the sheriff and asks, "Sheriff, should I head up to Story? I have a few hunches, and now that Al got these photos to us, I'm pretty sure I know who Pack Leader and Grinder are pretending to be and what they're driving."

Sheriff Manning expected that Jim would be anxious to get up there, but he had other plans for his deputy just then. "First thing I want you to do, Deputy, is head over to the hospital with those pictures and see if Marcy, the girl who was the survivor from the first attack up in Story, recognizes any of those faces. I'm headed up with our two highway patrolmen friends to follow up on some leads they had. If Marcy recognizes any of those faces, I want you to use the highway patrol radio tack system and let us know."

Manning stops and puts his hand on Jim's shoulder. "Linda is in classes all day at the junior college and your son is over at the day care right now, correct?" Jim nods his head. The sheriff continues. "I think it would be best if both of them stay down here in town until this all blows over. That Grinder is still probably carrying around a pretty big grudge with your name on it, and I don't want him using your family against you."

Jim can't help but feel grateful for the sheriff's concern for Linda and Jacob. "Yes, sir, I will head up to the hospital right now and talk with Marcy. If you guys need me at all, I'll carry the HP radio on my person."

The sheriff affectionately punches his deputy in the shoulder and tells him he'll call the college and leave a message for Linda to stay at his folks' house. He winks and says, "Now go get busy." When he walks to the squad car parking area, he waits for Jim to pull away before he goes over to talk to Joe and Jerry.

All three gather around the sheriff's Ford Bronco. Manning looks at Joe and asks, "You're positive that you saw Pack Leader and Grinder the way they look in those pictures?"

Joe pulls out two pictures from the manila envelope that Al gave him earlier and lays them on the hood of the Bronco. He points at them and says, "For the last couple of weeks, we have seen them driving around in a light blue VW van with Florida plates. First time we saw them was at the tavern where Marcy works, on the night of the attack. We didn't follow up on them the next day because she said they were attacked by bikers, and these guys all looked like a bunch of young, rich Easterners on a road trip. Are you sure that you don't want Jim with us on this? Half the sheriff's department and Sheridan Police Department are part of the National Guard and got activated with Al. Plus, most of the reinforcements sent up from Casper and Cheyenne are highway patrol. So we're all pretty short-handed right now."

The sheriff chuckles. "Al made me promise to try and keep Jim from running into Grinder before he's in custody. He says that Grinder knows how to push his buttons, and we all have seen what happens when those buttons get pushed. That's why he didn't let Jim see the pictures before now. But once he gets confirmation from Marcy of who those two are, he'll be up there in a flash. I'd say we got less than a couple of hours to get up there ourselves, arrest those bastards, and get them locked up."

Joe and Jerry agree and get on their bikes and lead Sheriff Manning up to Story.

Joe and his partner did a little surveillance of the two suspects in the '68 VW van and followed them to a storage barn about a mile south of the fish hatchery. That was where they saw the other identical van parked in back. They never could get a look inside the building but thought they had enough to go on with the pictures identifying Pack Leader and Grinder for a judge to issue a search warrant. Manning picked up the search warrant earlier that morning.

Wolves' Storage Building

Pack Leader knows he has to make his move today against Jim Edwards. He just does not see how that is going to happen. The phone on the wall rings twice, stops, and then rings twice again. Grinder looks up from working on his bike. "Boss, pigs are coming!"

Two years ago, Pack Leader decided that since Grinder went and got himself incarcerated, he had to have someone up here all the time to watch out for the operation back up on the mountain. So he set up his little network of "sleeper bikers." He paid these guys to stay up here all year round. Everyone in the gang had to do a year-long shift. Right now, between Sheridan and Story, there were fifteen guys who moved in and got jobs around the area to blend in with the local population. It was not necessary for them to clean up so much because Sheridan had a lot of biker wannabes who did their damnedest to look and act like the real thing.

Consequently, they had developed a good network of keeping everyone informed as to who and what was coming into Story at any given time. They used the phone system—one ring, hang up, and ring again meant pigs are at your door; two meant they're headed your way; and three meant answer the phone. He had already called in the eight from Sheridan, and they were with him and the original group he had brought on the hike last month. The other eight in Story were going to remain until after all the fireworks died down from the biker war that was about to explode in Sheridan County.

The phone rings three more times, stops, and rings three more. On the fourth ring, Pack Leader picks up.

"Okay, thanks, Bobby. Stay low. We'll call you if we need you." He hangs up, smiles, and looks at Grinder. "It's just Manning and our two HP biker buddies. This is how we're going to get Deputy Dog. We capture these guys, hide them at the camp, get him to come up, and then take him down there. We'll use Manning as leverage if things start to go south."

Seven of the men jump on the Harleys in the shed and head out the entrance toward the trail. Pack Leader and Grinder each take a van, getting in the driver's seat with the rest of the Wolves divided between the two vans. The noise from the seven Harley choppers is deafening as the guys rev up, because no one is using the muffler inserts. The bikers wait for the vans to go first and they follow. As they pull out onto the main road, they hear police sirens and look back to see two highway patrol Yamaha 350 patrol bikes followed by Manning's Ford Bronco.

Joe Mason looks over at Jerry Gibes and points to the seven choppers and two VW vans up in front of them and then points to the dirt road up ahead. Both men know that a normal van like that could not take on an unpaved mountain road for long, but they read Jim's report from the other day that said the vans are probably souped-up somehow. Jerry gives a thumbs-up, indicating that he understands, and then he looks back at the sheriff, who gives his own thumbs-up as well.

Manning clicks the loudspeaker button on his dash and orders the bikers to pull over. Instead of obeying, they all stick their middle fingers up and use their bikes to cover the entire road as they enter the unpaved part. Like a couple of NASCAR racing cars, both vans pull away from the biker group and race up in front and out of everyone's sight. The highway patrol has no way of getting to them. Manning tells them one more time to pull over or they will be forced to fire on them.

Just as he is getting his sidearm out of his holster, one of the vans comes out of the edge of the woods from a small horse trail and crashes into his Bronco. The impact is so sudden and hard that it smashes his door in and pushes him to the side and off the road. His left arm is broken by the impact and he loses control of his vehicle as it smashes against a big evergreen tree. When he looks up, he sees the bikers and some others on foot, surrounding his two highway patrol escorts and holding them at gunpoint.

Before anyone can get to him, he grabs his HP radio and says, "Jim, they bushwhacked us up on the old logging road behind the fish hatchery. Call Al and get some guardsmen up here stat." As he tries to repeat the message, he sees someone open the passenger door and they reach in and grab him, pulling him out of his truck.

Now lying on the ground, he looks up and sees a very clean-shaven Pack Leader standing over him with a .45 caliber 911 semiautomatic pointed at his head. "Believe it or not, Manning, you and your two girlfriends over there ain't going to die just yet. If that was your buddy Deputy Jim you were just talking to, I couldn't be happier. You see, the Wolves have a score to settle with that one and we want him up here too."

He can see by the look on the sheriff's face that he hit the nail on the head about trying to reach Jim. Then the radio chirps and Jim's voice comes over it. "Sheriff Manning, I got your message. Marcy just identified Pack Leader and Grinder from their military discharge photos. They're the ones who have been up there this whole time. They even came to my house once. Sheriff, they know where I live."

Pack Leader grabs the hand-held HP radio that he just heard Jim on. "Well, hey there, Deputy Jim. It was so nice talking to you and your lovely family the other day about fishing holes. We caught three big fish of our own right up here in your own back yard. If you want to see them again, I suggest you hightail it up here as fast as possible. And come alone or the sheriff gets a bullet in the head, then we tear into your other two friends."

Jim takes a calming breath as he sits in his squad car outside the Sheridan hospital. He knows that the bikers must have the sheriff, Joe, and Jerry, because that's the only way they could be talking on the highway patrol radio tack system.

"Where do you want to meet, biker?"

He hears Pack Leader's confiscated radio chirp into the frequency. "Well, now that we have a way of talking to one another, you just get up here within the hour; and once you get over by the Wagon Box, radio me."

Jim smiles because he knows that the local highway patrol is on the corner of Big Horn Avenue and East Brundage Lane on the south side of town, which is on the way to Story. "I'll be there as fast as I can. Don't hurt them!"

Grinder grabs the radio from Pack Leader and hollers, "Hurry up, cowshit, because once you get here, I'm going to rip your freaking head off and shit down your neck, then I'm...@#$... ouch! What the hell, Seth!"

Pack Leader grabs the radio from Grinder as he slaps the back of his head. "Give me that back, dipshit."

"Look, Jim, you just get here fast. I will know when you're where you're supposed to be, so don't hesitate to call me." He then turns off the radio for a second and glares at Grinder. "For one of the smartest sergeants I ever worked with in Nam, you are a real dumbass sometimes. You were just about ready to tell him how you were going to make your claim on his wife. What are you trying to do, get attacked by that damn bear again? We need to outthink him and kill him, period. No one's getting into some stupid *mano a mano* fight with that guy. We're going to put a bullet right between his eyes just like we did to that crazy kid in Nam."

Grinder rolls his eyes, gets right next to Pack Leader, and says in a very hushed voice, "Boss, these guys got to see me take him down. Otherwise, I'll never have their full respect again."

Pack Leader shakes his head and puts a hand on his friend's shoulder. "Todd, all we have to do is kill that stupid cowboy, and then you go have his wife and kill her and the kid. After that, no one will ever doubt you. Right now, I need you to go take care of the mountain road so that no guards can get up here. The rest of our boys should be in place over by Buffalo by now. They'll make their run through Sheridan and head up to the trucks on the reservation. That should keep the National Guard chasing their own tails until we can take care of Deputy Jim and his family and sneak out the same way we came in. I'll take Manning and the two HPs with me to the camp and wait. When the deputy gets to the Wagon Box, we'll lure him up and kill him. Then I'll contact you and you can go take care of his family."

With that, Grinder gets a big grin on his face, throws back his head, and lets out a loud wolf call. Pack Leader and the rest of the men follow suit.

While the two bikers are talking over him, Sheriff Manning is about to have a panic attack at the thought that he never got a chance to warn Linda Edwards not to come up to Story after her college classes let out. He can only pray that Jim decided to check on her and Jacob.

Chapter Thirteen
Now You Did It, Ya Went and Let the Bear Out!

Linda and Jacob Driving to Story

Linda doesn't know why she feels nervous as she's driving Jim's truck up to Story this afternoon, but she does. She looks behind her and sees that her husband still has his dad's old shotgun hanging on the rack in the back window and decides to take it into the house with her. She knows something big is going on because earlier that day when she was standing outside at the campus, she saw about two dozen National Guard trucks towing heavy military guns heading south on I-90 toward Buffalo.

She pulls up to their place and Thunder, who is on his leash tied up to his doghouse on the side of the cabin, immediately starts barking. Full-grown now, he weighs one hundred pounds, and she swears he looks more wolf than dog. But to her, Jim, Jacob, friends, and family he was the kindest and gentlest dog they had ever owned. The only time he looked like a mad wolf was when those two tourists came to the door the other day asking about fishing holes.

Jacob gets out of the truck and starts to run to the back yard, and his mother tells him to get Thunder and bring him in the house. When she gets inside, the phone rings and she can tell it's for her because each member on the party line has a slightly different ring. She runs over and picks up the phone. Jim is on the end of the line.

"Linda, honey, it's Jim. Listen, those two who showed up to the house looking for fishing holes are the two bikers we're looking for. They have their gang hiding out somewhere in Story and they know where we live. I need you to get Jacob and get out of there now. I am over at the Wagon Box about ready to radio the bikers. I stopped at the HP building on Brundage and was able to get a message sent to Al, who is on I-90. He'll cut a squad off from his Guard unit and will be heading up shortly."

Before Jim can say another word, there is a big explosion and a slight tremor felt all over town. Linda asks Jacob what's going on, but he's clueless. Someone then cuts into the party line call. "Linda, it's Mary from down the street. My husband just said that a big tractor trailer coming up the mountain on 93 was over-turned by an explosion. He says that there are some National Guardsmen trying to move it, but someone else is shooting at them. Is Jim here in Story?"

Jim gulps. "Mary, I'm right here at the Wagon Box. Al just had a fight with those boys on I-90 and now he's headed up here. That's the unit he sent ahead. The boys firing on them must be some more of the Wild Wolves gang. Linda, maybe you should head over to Mary's place until I can get over there."

Mary says, "Jim, that ain't going to work. We're in the basement now. There are stray bullets flying all over the place over here. Linda is safer where she is at."

One Hour Earlier, Interstate I-90, Sheridan County Border

Al knows that in combat you pay attention to everything, and especially anything that just does not look quite normal. He has seen ten food supply trucks roll by in the last three hours and all of them were riding high and empty. Normally, food suppliers don't roll into Montana empty and then fill up. Just the opposite. Ten in a row is too much for his jarhead mind to deal with. He radios the National Guard HQ and tells them to inform his buddy, Lieutenant Bill Roberts up in Billings, about what is going on and to have the Montana Highway Patrol check it out.

While he is finishing his conversation, one of his staff sergeants yells, "Sergeant Major, about one hundred bikes at twelve o'clock, five miles out!" Al takes his binoculars and focuses in on the group. At the top of a hill on I-90 just before you hit city limits, Al sees them. Every man that he can see is armed with assault rifles or shotguns, and it looks like some are carrying grenades. Al has his equipment lined up on one side under camouflage. The only thing visible is himself, about twenty-five armed soldiers, and two trucks behind him.

As the bikers approach, Al has his twenty-five soldiers line up on either side of him, and he steps forward. He is not one to break with regulations, but he had gotten so used to his .357 duty pistol that he just plain forgot to strap on his regulation .45 caliber 911 semiautomatic sidearm that day. Besides, the .357 is a lot more comfortable to wear.

Over the roar of the idling bikes, he addresses a big Latino man in front, whom he recognizes as one of Pack Leader's top lieutenants. "You must be that dipshit they call Demolisher. Never did like you demolition pussies. Always blowing shit up from a safe distance."

Demolisher uses the movement of getting off his Harley to conceal the fact that he just grabbed a grenade off a loop on the back of his jeans. "You must be that loud-mouthed Marine Corps jarhead everyone is so scared of. If you ask me, *hombre*, you look like a little weasel with no hair."

As he is talking, he reaches behind and unpins his grenade and brings it around to throw it. Al did not live this long by being stupid or blind. Before Demolisher can throw the grenade, Al quick draws his .357, and shoots Demolisher in the head. The grenade drops out of his hand and at the same time Al dives for the ground and yells "FIRE!"

All at once, the twenty-five men behind him and the sixty-some on the side of the road in the hidden machinegun nests open fire on the bikers. Each guardsman barely gets two or three rounds off before Al calls out, "Ceasefire!"

Three Harleys manage to get around Al's group and nick a couple of guardsmen before they take off up I-90. When the dust settles, barely half of the Wolves are still on their bikes and breathing. They all have already thrown their guns to the ground and have their hands on their heads.

Al tells his sergeants to get the area policed up as he heads back to call for emergency medical and prisoner transportation. While on the radio with the National Guard HQ, he gets the message from Jim about Sheriff Manning and the two highway patrolmen being held prisoner up in Story by Pack Leader and Grinder. He puts his hand over the mic and yells at a corporal, who is also a highway patrolman, to take a transport of ten men and head up to Story to assist Jim. He tells the guy to drop by the Guard armory and grab his HP radio so he can talk to Jim. He tells his contact at the Guard to relay a message to Jim that help is coming and to stay put until they get there.

Al is nervous as hell now because he knows that if Jim thinks the sheriff and those two boys are in too much trouble, the first life he'll sacrifice to save them will be his own. Panic goes through him as another thought hits his brain. He runs over to a Jeep that's on the side of the road, looks at a private standing by it, and tells him he'll be right back. He heads up to the first exit into Sheridan and runs into a gas station, and without asking he barges behind the desk and calls the community college. Panic again goes across his face as he finds out that Linda Edwards went over to the campus day care and picked up Jacob and headed up to Story about an hour ago.

It takes him about an hour to wrap things up with the Guard to the point that he can get another transport and head to Story. By that time, he already knows that a tractor trailer has been blown up on 93 and that no one knows where Jim is. The corporal and his men that he sent up earlier are pinned down behind the truck wreckage and are in a firefight with some bikers.

He does, however, get in touch with Linda and knows that she is safe, at least for now. He has only one option—to get up to his men and fight his way through and go find Jim before he does something really stupid.

Back Up in Story

Jim's radio chirps. "Deputy Jim, where are you?"

Jim picks up the radio on his car seat. "I'm right where you told me to be. Now what?"

"Now I want you to go up to the fish hatchery and take that old logging road about three miles up, and then go up that hiking trail that leads into the park for another two miles. We'll be waiting for you."

Jim rolls his eyes. "Well, my squad car can make it up the logging road okay, but it'll never make it up that hiking trail. If I have to hike up it, I won't be there for a couple of hours."

"You see, that's what I like about you, Deputy Jim. We both think alike. So to save you that turmoil, I left you one of the forest service's three-wheel Mazda T2000 trucks that we commandeered earlier today at the beginning of the trail. We've used it a couple times to haul supplies, and it does just fine on that trail."

"Okay, I have to get some gas, because I'm about to run out. So I'll be there in an hour."

"Any longer and we start carving pieces out of your three buddies up here. Okay, Deputy?"

Jim says okay and sets the radio down. He has to think fast, because he knows Linda is over at the house and he just does not feel like he can focus until he knows she is safe. His mother-in-law had an old bomb shelter in the backyard that was built by the previous owners.

He drives over to his house and gets Linda, Jacob, and Thunder in there and has her seal it up. Fortunately, they cleaned it out last fall and were planning on making it into some kind of guest quarters in the future. There really aren't any supplies in there anymore, but Linda grabs enough food and water to last a couple of days before she goes in. Jim is glad she grabbed his dad's shotgun out of the truck earlier. It holds three shots and one in the chamber. He gives her a box of 12-gauge big-game shot and lets her lock up.

Next, he goes in the house and calls Phil Morganson, the owner of a local horse rental facility. "Phil, its Deputy Jim Edwards. I have an emergency. Can you get me a good trail horse that you can spare, and maybe even do without? I'm going to need him to get the sheriff and the highway patrol guys away from a gang of bikers, and there could be a lot of fireworks, if you know what I mean." Jim tells Phil where to meet him in twenty minutes and hangs up.

It takes him about fifteen minutes to get up to the beginning of the trail that Pack Leader told him to take the T2000 up. When he arrives, he is followed by a Ford F100 pickup truck pulling a horse trailer. Jim gets out, walks around his patrol car, and opens up the trunk. He pulls out a riot helmet, bulletproof vest, and a brand-new Mossberg 500 police 12-gauge shotgun. Specifically designed for law enforcement, it has an extended magazine that can hold seven shells with one in the chamber, which gives the carrier eight shots before he has to reload. On the side of the butt is a leather pouch that has six slots to store extra shells. He puts on his gear and walks over to the horse trailer.

Phil Morganson has been renting horses in Story for over twenty years now, mainly to tourists but sometimes to ranchers for work. Once in a great while, Wyoming law enforcement would rent when they needed to go up into high country for special jobs. He brings one of the horses that has some experience, a twelve-year-old Appaloosa named Freeway.

He gets the last piece of equipment on Freeway and looks up to see Jim approaching. Jim smiles and grabs Phil's extended hand. "Thanks, Phil. Al and the Guard are tied up on 93 with that overturned truck. Right now they're in a firefight with some bikers. The rest of the gang has the sheriff, Joe, and Jerry up there. I'm going to lead this horse up the trail with that three-wheeler over there and then take him and try to rescue them. It could go bad and the horse could get hurt."

While he is talking, he looks at the horse a little closer. He sees that the animal has a special covering over its head and front torso. He points at it and asks what it is for.

"That's called horse riot gear. When I started renting to law enforcement, Al put me in touch with some people who could get me this stuff. It's lightweight and bulletproof to a degree. Freeway here will at least have a fighting chance of surviving what you're taking him into." Phil turns around and goes to the trailer and grabs a long lead rope. He attaches it to Freeway's halter and hands Jim the end. "This should give you enough room between you and him so he doesn't spook over being led by that contraption."

He walks up to the horse and rubs the side of his head affectionately. "You come out of this alive and well, you hear me? Now go be a hero and bring this boy and our friends home." Phil leans in, hugs the horse, and pats him on the neck, then looks at Jim. "You take care, kid. I'll make some phone calls and see if we can't help Al out up here somehow."

The two men shake hands and Phil gets in his truck and drives off. Jim reaches down to his hip and grabs the highway patrol radio. "I'm here, Pack Leader. Heading up now."

"Thanks for the heads-up, Deputy. Looking forward to seeing you. We'll be listening for the three-wheeler."

Jim walks over to his car one more time, grabs a roll of duct tape, and sticks it with his gear. He gets in the vehicle, starts it, and takes off with Freeway in tow. The Mazda T2000 looks like a regular truck, but is much smaller and only has three wheels. The park rangers use them to haul supplies from one area to another over small trails.

It takes Jim and the horse about twenty minutes to get up to the point on the trail that he wanted to get to before entering the camp. He leaves the T2000 running and transfers all his gear from the three-wheeler onto Freeway. He periodically sticks his foot in the driver's side of the vehicle and slowly revs the throttle so it sounds like he's still moving. He then takes the duct tape and jerry-rigs the steering wheel so that it won't turn.

He knows that the camp is less than a quarter mile up the trail, which fortunately is fairly straight and flat into the camp. He then tapes up the throttle so that it will not go any faster than ten miles an hour. He slowly gets out, puts the vehicle in drive, and lets it go straight up the trail toward the camp. Then he runs over and mounts Freeway and takes off to his left toward a wooded gully beside the camp. To his great delight, Freeway lives up to his name and very quickly gallops through the gully and gets him behind the camp before the T2000 makes it far enough for the bikers to see it.

When he stops, he can see eight men spread out around the entrance of the camp where he's supposed to be coming in. They are all armed and waiting to ambush him. He spots Sheriff Manning over by the campfire. He looks pretty banged up and his left arm is definitely broken. It also looks like no one bothered to tie him up because of how banged up he is, but Joe and Jerry are tied up together around a tree across from Manning. They look a little banged up too, but not as bad as the sheriff.

One of the bikers in front yells, "Pack Leader, that truck is empty! It just ran into a tree!"

Someone else yells, "Go check it out!"

The two in front get up and scamper down the trail.

Jim thanks God that the T2000 made it that far. He reaches down and grabs the Mossberg 500 shotgun, pumps a shell in, and puts another back in the cylinder so that he has eight shots. He puts the horse's reins in his mouth, bites down, and boots Freeway in the ribs and yells, "Go!"

Before any of the bikers can respond, Jim shoots the two who are closest to him dead-center as the horse thunders through the camp. With the shotgun in one hand, he reaches in his jacket pocket and throws a four-inch hunting knife to Joe and Jerry that fortunately lands close enough to Jerry's hands for him to grab it. When he passes the sheriff, he pulls his .357 revolver out and tosses it down to him. Manning grabs it with his good hand. Jim sees four more bikers ready to fire at him, so he pumps a round into three of them. The fourth disappears into the woods.

He yanks back on the reins with his head and Freeway comes to a stop. He looks around for the three men who are still missing and is about to head down the trail when he hears a gunshot and feels a huge impact against the side of his head as he falls over sideways onto the ground. Disoriented, he reaches his hand up to his helmet and feels the spot where the bullet hit. The dent is about a half-inch deep, and he tries to shake the ringing out of his ears. He manages to get on his feet when he finally sees the dark-haired tourist who visited him at his house the other day standing a couple feet away with a .45-caliber pointed at him.

Pack Leader smiles and shakes his head. "I'll say one thing, Deputy Jim, you're full of surprises. But in the end what they'll say is 'Pack Leader took that deputy out,' and that's what they'll remember." He raises the gun and points it right at Jim's face, laughs, and starts to pull the trigger.

A gunshot sounds and the .45 is knocked out of his hand.

Both Jim and the biker are stunned and look over to see Sheriff Manning half standing, half leaning against a tree with Jim's .357 in his hand. Manning is having trouble steadying the gun he is holding. He looks at Jim. "Damn it, I hate being left-eye dominant. Shit, Jim, I was aiming for his stupid head."

Before he can say another word, shots start flying from the trail south of the camp that the other two bikers went down earlier. The sheriff finds cover behind the tree and starts to return fire. Pack Leader yells, "Get up here and kill these ass-holes. Now!"

As he is yelling, Jim barrels into him like a raging bull and pushes him across the camp and out of range of the gunfight now raging between the sheriff and the two bikers.

Jim knows he has to take Pack Leader out quickly, before he can get to another weapon and help his men. He rams the hard helmet on his head straight into Pack Leader's jaw as he comes up. The impact knocks him back and down. But as Jim comes forward, a boot shoots up into his face and Pack Leader jumps to his feet. Jim reaches up and pulls a tooth from his mouth and throws it on the ground. Pack Leader looks at it and then spits out one of his own, laughs, then steps in and starts to pummel Jim with powerhouse punches.

As the biker's sledgehammers are landing against his arms and sides, he can't help but think that Pack Leader hits like the state champ Richard Ladenza, and that gives him an idea.

Jim ducks down low, moves in under the attack and starts pummeling Pack Leader's midsection. The punches aren't as powerful as the biker's, but they're three times faster and he proceeds to jackhammer Pack Leader back until he is propped up against a tree.

All the biker can do now is play the rope-a-dope and look for an opening. He thinks he sees one when he tries to knee Jim in the groin, but that assault is met by a straight downward punch to his thigh that hurts so much it causes him to lean harder on the tree and put most of his weight on the other foot.

Jim knows that there won't be any bell to stop this fight, and he's worried that Sheriff Manning is outgunned, and Joe and Jerry are not yet free to help him. The area where he and Pack Leader are fighting is heavy with trees and large boulders. He knows there is a big boulder behind him and he gets another idea. Al taught him some Marine Corps hand-to-hand combat techniques that included some judo. One of his favorite moves was what he liked to call "The Errol Flynn move."

He rams a couple more fists into Pack Leader's gut, head-butts him again, places his right hand around the back of his head, jams his right foot into Pack Leader's midsection, crouches, and rolls onto his back with the biker balanced on his foot. At just the right time in the roll, he thrusts his right leg out and forward, catapulting Pack Leader into the air almost eight feet off the ground and into the ten-foot-high boulder behind him. Pack Leader flies into it upside down. When he lands, his head hits the boulder first, and his neck breaks before he hits the dirt.

Jim looks back, sees the contorted way Pack Leader landed and guesses the man is dead.

As he gets up to go help the sheriff and the highway patrolmen, he sees that Joe and Jerry are already up, and they have the other two bikers on their knees and in handcuffs. One of the bikers looks at his friend. "Did you see that? He beat the shit out of Pack Leader and killed him with his bare hands. Who the hell is this guy?"

The other biker just shakes his head. "Yeah, and before that, he rides in here on a horse and takes out half the crew before we know what hit us. Geez, man, we're the lucky ones."

Despite all his injuries, Sheriff Manning manages to get up and go help Jim. He hands him back his duty pistol and tells him that he's the only guy besides Al and himself who really owns his gun in the department, and he'd not think of keeping it for another second. He tells Jim that Joe and Jerry used the knife he threw them to cut themselves loose, retrieved their duty pistols from where the bikers had put them and circled around to the back of the two bikers on the trail. There they easily captured and subdued them.

Joe Mason walks up to Jim and grabs him around the head and pulls his forehead to his shoulder in a brotherly embrace. "Dude, I have never seen anything like that in my life. If I had known you were this tough, I definitely would have gotten you to play football on the Broncs team with us. With you, we just might have beat Natrona in that state championship."

They both hear a big gasp and turn to see Jerry standing there with the prisoners. He laughs, looks at Jim, and gives him a thumbs-up. "Thanks Jim. You saved all of us."

Jim tells the sheriff what is going on in Story and how some more bikers have Al's guardsmen pinned down on 93 coming up the mountain. Joe and Jerry decide that they'll help the sheriff down the trail. Joe takes the T2000, ties the lead rope to the two handcuffed prisoners and fastens it to the vehicle, then helps Manning into the passenger seat. Jerry climbs in back to watch the prisoners, and Joe drives. Meanwhile, Jim grabs Freeway and gallops back to his squad car on the logging road.

One thing that starts bothering Jim is that the blond-haired guy they all know now as Grinder was not with the group up at the camp. Even though he knows that Linda and Jacob are pretty safe in the shelter, he just feels that he has to get home.

When he gets back to his car, he radios the guys still back on the trail and tells them he's going home to check on Linda and Jacob. He leaves Freeway tied up next to the trail and takes off. Joe told him that he would find Phil Morganson and return Freeway and then go get the other highway patrol bike to see if he could get some help for Al.

It takes Jim about twenty minutes to get to his house from the camp in his squad car. When he does, he goes to the shelter and raps on the door in a predetermined signal he and Linda came up with earlier. The metal door unlatches and opens, and Linda, Jacob, and Thunder all barrel out of there and into Jim's arms at once. Thunder is so excited to be out of there that he starts running around the backyard and chasing his tail. Of course, Jacob starts to chase the dog, and Linda has to calm both of them down as they go inside.

Once inside, Jim gives Linda a brief synopsis of what happened up at the biker camp. He does his best to downplay any risks he took, and he didn't explain how he took down Pack Leader. Linda is no dummy. She just figures that she'll get all the gaps filled in by the sheriff and the highway patrol boys later.

"We need to get out of Story, and if we have to, we'll just hike down to Sheridan," Jim says.

While he is talking, he hears several loud motorcycles pull up to the house. He looks out the corner of the front window and sees Grinder with ten others sitting out on the street and in his driveway. Grinder gets off his bike and walks up to the gate and yells, "Mrs. Edwards, I am sorry to inform you that you are now a widow. But that's okay, 'cause I'm going to take your husband's place and let you know what it's like to have a real man."

One Hour Earlier, Highway 93, Mountain Pass into Story

Al knows he has to get into Story as fast as possible. Manning is the commanding-officer type and can lay out a good battle plan, dot all the i's and cross the t's, but when it comes to execution, he needs a man like Al to make it happen. The two highway patrol bikers are good stock, and with some more experience will turn into some damn fine lawmen. Jim, on the other hand, is a bit of a lawman prodigy; but if things go south, he's going to take on everything by himself and probably get killed in the process. That is something Al refuses to let happen.

The only thing standing in his way is this damn overturned truck and those asshole bikers up there taking potshots at his men. He looks around at his resources and decides that he is not going to risk any of these fifteen weekend warrior soldiers' lives by making a frontal assault up the road. He figures that there are at least fifteen to twenty bikers up there with what looks like everything from .45 caliber pistols and shotguns to .30-30 hunting rifles. Luckily, none of the resources the bikers had out on I-90 seem to have made it to these guys, so he doesn't feel like he's going to have to deal with grenades or assault rifles.

He takes a good look at his terrain, walks around the bend out of gunshot range of the bikers, and looks at the cliff wall that goes up to the next level of the road. It's only about fifty feet high, and the bikers won't come over there because Al's men could take them out pretty easily. No, they have to stay on the road and guard that entrance. He could take five boys and scale that wall and tell his other soldiers to attack up the hill at the same time as he attacks from behind. It would be a much more effective strategy, but he could still lose some soldiers, and to Al that is still not good enough. He needs a distraction.

His radio chirps. "Lieutenant Freeburger, are you on this channel? It's Highway Patrolman Joe Mason, sir."

Al grabs the HP radio sitting on his Jeep seat. "It's Sergeant Major Freeburger right now, Joe, and yes, I am here. What the hell is going on up there and where is your partner, Sheriff Manning, and Jim?"

"Sergeant Major, you're not going to believe this, but the sheriff, Jerry, and I were captured by Pack Leader and his bikers. The sheriff got pretty banged up and they took us up to their camp above the old logging road by the fish hatchery. Pack Leader used us to lure Jim up there to kill him. Only, Jim did some luring of his own. He rode a horse into camp and killed five bikers, then got in a fight with Pack Leader and killed him with his bare hands. It was the damnedest thing any of us ever saw."

Al replies, "Were there any bikers that survived?"

"Yes. Jerry and I were able to capture two of them, and he and the sheriff are bringing them down as we speak."

Shit, Al thinks to himself. Now everyone is going to know about Jim's little show. He asks Joe where he is and what is he doing right now. Joe tells him about the horse named Freeway that Jim rode in on and how he's taking him back to the owner. He just now got to his abandoned bike and got his radio to call in.

As Joe is telling Al these details, a very devious grin creases Al's face as an idea pops into his head. "Joe, keep that horse in its riot gear and contact Phil Morganson. See if you can get him to bring that horse and some others over here in a trailer, and you follow over on your bike. I think you just made it easy for us to get up this mountain without losing any of my men."

Twenty minutes later, Al and five soldiers are scaling that cliff wall and the ten others are around the corner waiting for his orders to attack. He gets to the top and peers over at the bikers who are all fanned out on the road, taking cover behind abandoned cars and trucks. In the back and farther up, he sees a blond-haired man, clean-shaven and sporting a crew cut, whom he's sure is Grinder. With him are ten others on bikes.

While about eight bikers are on the road in a firefight with the guardsmen, Grinder and his ten are pushing their bikes away from the area. Al looks over at the corporal next to him on the wall. "That coward is abandoning his men over there and sneaking off." He takes his radio and turns it way down and puts it to his ear. "Joe, where the hell are you? Grinder is wussing out and trying to run."

"Sergeant Major, we're still a couple minutes away. Don't worry—if he's headed up to the camp, he's in for a sorry surprise. He has nowhere to go. We'll get him." Al knows in his gut that Grinder is going to make a stop on his way, and because of that, he and his soldiers need to make this a very quick operation.

Five minutes later, Joe gets on the radio and tells Al he's ready. Al smiles and says, "Go." At that moment, a highway patrol Yamaha 350 Enduro motorcycle flies over the cliff into the area where the eight abandoned bikers are. Then five horseman all dressed in riot gear and sporting shotguns charge down the road and start firing into the bikers. Al and his five men jump up on the road with automatic assault rifles and he with his .357 duty pistol. The soldiers who were farther down the hill charge up with their rifles pointed at the totally astonished bikers.

The Wild Wolves on the road see that their backup has abandoned them, and all the fight is drained out of them at the sensory overload spectacle they are witnessing. All eight men throw their weapons to the ground, put their hands on top of their heads and kneel down.

It takes Al about ten terrible minutes to get everyone and everything in order before he can leave. He looks over at Joe. "I'm taking you and the five boys who came up the cliff with me and we're going to go get Grinder and his boys."

Phil Morganson tells him they can use his truck to carry everyone.

Joe looks over at Al. "You think he's headed up to the camp?"

Al gets a grim look on his face. "No. He is headed over to Jim's place, and that is exactly where we needed to be five minutes ago."

Al and Joe get the soldiers situated in the back of Phil's truck. Al walks over to Phil and shakes his hand. "That was one hell of a risk you and your friends took for us, Phil. I can't tell you how much that means to me."

Phil smiles and slaps Al on the shoulder. "Ah, hell, Al, just doing our part. Just remember that if any law enforcement around here ever needs horses you tell them where to rent them, okay?" Al smiles and assures Phil that as long as he is sucking air and wearing a badge, that will be a given.

As the truck rounds a corner near Jim and Linda's place, the people in it can hear high-caliber pistol fire coming from inside the house, and then a huge explosion happens on the far side in the driveway that goes to the shed in back. As they get closer, Al and his people hear more gun and shotgun fire.

What they see next, Al could only later describe as Jim looking like Conan the Barbarian on his porch, swinging a shotgun around like a battle axe, bashing bikers' heads in. His front lawn is littered with dead and unconscious bikers. Jim's dog, Thunder, has one man pinned up against a tree with his jaws fastened on the man's crotch, looking up at the man's petrified face, growling menacingly.

Chapter Fourteen
This Ones on You Biker!

Ten Minutes Earlier, Jim's House

Jim goes cold for a moment as he realizes what that monster just said. He quickly takes Linda and Jacob back to their bedroom and hands her his duty pistol. He takes his son into the bathroom and puts him in the bathtub and tells Thunder to guard them. "I don't think that stray fire can make it through any of these log walls, Linda, but better safe than sorry. You watch that door and shoot anyone but me who comes through it. I'll do what I can to keep them out until help arrives."

Jim thinks about taking them back to the shelter but he knows they might be seen from the front yard and decides not to take the risk. He grabs both shotguns and makes sure they are fully loaded. He knows that he has only twelve shots between the two of them, so he's going to have to make them count. Everything inside of him wants to explode with rage and go out there and kill as many of the bikers as he can, but that conversation with Al at the diner keeps coming back to him. He knows he won up at the biker camp because he kept his cool and used his head. He also knows that Al should be getting into Story pretty soon, and no biker gang wants to take on a real army. With this logic in his mind, he begins to calm down and decides to give them one chance to stand down. They think he's dead, so confronting them alive just might scare the hell out of them enough to make them surrender.

A bolt of ice-cold panic goes up and down Grinder's spine as Deputy Jim Edwards of the Sheridan County Sheriff's Department steps out on the porch of his log cabin house with two shotguns in his hands aimed right at him. With the same hard stare that reminded him of the bear, the deputy yells, "The National Guard took down your gang out on I-90 and is headed up here with over one hundred soldiers and equipment. They're armed to the teeth and you boys don't have a chance. We know about your camp north of town and how you all got here without being noticed. We already took down Pack Leader and the bikers up there, so no one is coming to help you, Grinder. Stand down now and no one needs to die."

Grinder feels so humiliated by this Boy Scout deputy that he forgets about how scared he is. He pulls out his 911 pistol. "The only one who is going to die here, cowshit, is you, and then your wife and kid. But not until I go show her a really good time."

As Grinder takes aim, Jim gets one shot off before he hits the floor and takes cover behind the thick concrete and log half-wall on his porch. The bullets start to fly as all of Grinder's men unload on Jim's house. Jim's blood rushes to his temples and his heart starts to race a mile a second. His teeth start to chatter as he yells, "I told you what would happen the next time you threatened my wife and son, biker. This one is on you!"

Jim's porch has two four-foot-wide concrete pillars that go from the porch half-wall to the roof overhang. He jumps up behind the one closest to the porch entrance with his duty shotgun in hand and yells, "YOU BASTARDS, STAY THE HELL AWAY FROM MY WIFE AND SON!" He then unloads three blasts of shotgun shells like they were machinegun rounds and takes out the three bikers nearest to the porch. With that, the other eight bikers immediately jump for cover anywhere they can find it. Jim rolls around the pillar to the other side and shoots three more bikers. He only has six more shots and there are still five bikers left. In the next few seconds, Jim expends the rest of the ammo in his duty shotgun and grabs his dad's. He does manage to get one more biker but loses count of how many shots he has left.

Meanwhile, Linda and Jacob are huddled in the bathroom tub. Jacob asks his mom what all the noise is, and she lies and tells him that daddy is watching a John Wayne movie on TV and has the volume too loud. She immediately adds that it is too late for him to go watch it with him. When he asks why they are huddling in the tub, she has no answer; so she just tells him to pet Thunder, which he does.

Grinder can see that Jim has much better cover to fight from than he and his men, so he motions at the biker closest to him. "I'm going around to the side of the house to try to get a good shot at him. It has to be me who kills him. Keep him pinned down, and when I give the signal all of you go." The other Wolf nods and starts to fire.

Grinder puts his muffler insert on his bike and starts it up. He sees that Jim does not notice him as he slinks around to the other side while his men have Jim pinned down. He gets in position but knows he needs Jim to stand up before he can get a good shot. The biker he was just talking to is looking straight at him as he waves to go.

Jim hears the men rushing up to the porch, and stands and starts firing. He gets two right away. Inside the house, Linda and Jacob are still in the bathroom but something out the window on the far side of the room catches her attention. When she looks closer, she can see that it is a motorcycle, and the blond-haired man that visited them the other day is sitting on it with a gun in his hand, about ready to fire. She looks over at Jacob and tells him that there is a wolf outside trying to get in, so she is going to shoot it and tells him to not be afraid. She grabs Jim's pistol and aims at the gas tank of the bike and fires two shots. The second one hits just right and causes the tank to explode right between the biker's legs, propelling Grinder up and back onto the driveway.

Meanwhile, Out on the Porch

Jim is in a very serious situation with three bikers advancing on him and yelling, "Grinder, take the shot!" When the explosion happens, Jim rushes the bikers with his now empty shotgun and smashes the first in the face with the butt end. When he goes down, the next one tries to raise his gun to shoot Jim, but to everyone's amazement Thunder jumps through the already demolished living room window and knocks the man over the porch wall and onto the front yard. The biker loses his gun when the dog attacks. He has no recourse but to back up against a tree as Thunder places his very large and very sharp teeth right on his crotch and proceeds to growl at him.

Now only two bikers are left. Both are dumbfounded as they stare at Jim's dog and his capture of their buddy for a moment and then collect their wits and turn back to attack Jim.

Jim sees the move and grabs the shotgun by the barrel and proceeds to pummel both men, knocking one out immediately. He sees that the other can barely stand, so he takes the butt end of his dad's shotgun and rams it into his face, knocking him over the porch wall and onto the lawn. With no one conscious or alive but the guy pinned by Thunder on the lawn, Jim leans against one of the pillars and wipes the sweat and blood out of his eyes. When he looks up, he notices a pickup truck in front of his house, and sees Al Freeburger, Joe Mason, and five guardsmen coming up his lawn.

Al walks onto the porch and over to Jim and puts both hands on the young man's shoulders. "You okay, kid?"

Jim drops his head and shakes it while trying to steady himself. "I'll live, Al, but I think I'm going to reconsider my career choices."

Al takes off his guardsman hat, rubs his hand across the top of his head, and says, "I'm going to have to agree with you on that one, kid."

"So do I."

Everyone turns around to see Linda in the doorway with Jim's gun in her hand. Joe and Al step away as Linda comes out and inspects her husband. She places an affectionate hand on the side of his cheek and sighs. "You look like hell." She looks around the front yard at all the bodies, and then back at Jim. "I do not want our son to see all this death."

She lays the pistol on the porch wall and puts both hands on the side of his face and pulls it right in front of her nose. "He will never know what went on here. You have to promise me that, Jim Edwards, okay?"

Jim sighs and says that he will never talk about this day to Jacob. Linda starts to cry and falls into her husband's arms. They both walk into their home to take care of their son and clean up.

Chapter Fifteen
A Different Path

One Week Later, Sheriff Manning's Office

"Damn it, George, I won't back down on this. That kid does not need to wear a badge anymore."

"Al, I don't get it. He's the best we've seen or ever had. In ten years, he could be sheriff. I already told him he'd have my support, and he should have yours too."

"No!"

"Why the hell not?"

"Look, George, I like you and you're one of the best COs I've served under in combat. You're a damn good sheriff too. But you haven't seen what I have. Men like Jim Edwards are like secret weapons. You use them when nothing else works. But if you use them too long and too hard, sooner or later they end up dead. That kid took down almost twenty bikers single-handedly. He has been seen beating the crap out of two of the toughest bikers in the country. One he killed with his bare hands. If he stays in uniform, every Pack Leader and Grinder wannabe from New York to San Francisco is going to come up here and test themselves against him. Sooner or later, one of them is going to get lucky, and then you and I are going to have to explain why we let that happen to a devastated widow and son."

George leans forward and points a finger at Al. "What about you and that stunt you pulled out there on the highway with that 'Wild Bill Hickok' quick-draw sharpshooting shit. Ain't that going to get some of those bikers coming after you?"

"If they do, they'll get an army rammed up their asses, and I think they know it. I work with a team, George, you know that. I had the whole Guard standing behind me when I did that. You don't need to worry about me one bit."

George leans back in his chair and sighs. "Damn it, Al, I don't know how many more years I can do this. You ain't no spring chicken either. What are we supposed to do? Die as old men in this department? Maybe I would like to spend some nice retirement years with someone. Go see the country or something."

Al relaxes and chuckles. "For crying out loud, George, there isn't a decent woman in this whole damn county who would put up with either one of us. Plus, when you were active duty, you saw half the world. What more do you want? I got my daughter, Pearl, and you have your own kids. Let's just keep plugging away until we can't. When that day comes, I betcha the Almighty will just go and get us another good sheriff."

"So what's Jim and his family going to do now, Al? They really can't stay around here. Even if you did erase all the official records, people are going to talk."

Al winks and chuckles. "You remember that private I told you about who I had back during the big one in '45? The one who said he's going home to Alabama to make a million after the war?"

"Yes, he called himself JR or something. What about him?"

"Well, he made more than a million over the last thirty years. He has the biggest new car dealership owner in Alabama. He's looking for someone to run his body shop and detail shop down there. I gave him a recommendation about Jim. He called back yesterday and said he would pay for Jim's move and get him set up in a nice rental and everything. They leave next week."

Sheriff Manning just shakes his head and laughs. "You know, Al, with all your connections I sometimes wonder why the hell you aren't a millionaire by now."

Al shakes his head and gives George a sideways smirk. "What the hell would I do with all that crap? First thing you know, fifty-plus shirttail relatives would come out of the woodwork looking for a handout. Not this marine. I'm just fine living on the pittance I get from you and having a daughter who's willing to put up with me from time to time."

Jim, Linda, Jacob, and Thunder do move to Alabama that year and Jim starts out as the detail shop/body shop manager for JR's dealership in Birmingham. After eight years, Jim is JR's chief operational officer for all his Birmingham dealerships.

JR then offers Jim an opportunity he could not turn down. The automotive entrepreneur set his sights on a quickly growing auto auction in south central Pennsylvania called Manheim Auto Auction. JR wants to start sending the majority of the used car trade-ins from all his dealerships that he did not want to keep on his lots to that auction. He offers to finance Jim in starting up his own auto reconditioning and auction service business there.

Much to his surprise, Jim and Linda do not need any loans to get started. After selling the house in Story, the property in New York State, plus their aggressive savings plan, they have enough to move to Manheim and open up their business. Jim just makes sure that JR will keep him supplied with fresh work every week, which JR is more than willing to do—and did, up to the day he died.

In 1987, after graduating from the United States Merchant Marine Academy in Long Island, New York, Jacob Edwards is commissioned into the United States Coast Guard. You know the rest of the story!

Epilogue

Present Day, Rainbow Bar, Sheridan, Wyoming

When Joe is done speaking, he sees that Jim's son, Jacob, is standing behind his dad rubbing his shoulders. Jim has his arm around his granddaughter, Danielle, while she has her head leaning against his chest. Both Jacob and Danielle are crying. Little Roberto climbs down from his mother's lap, crawls into his grandfather's lap and gives him a hug. Joe takes a deep breath, raises his beer and says, "Here's to my friend, Jim Edwards. One of Sheridan's finest." Everyone in the bar raises their drinks and joins the toast.

As the crowd breaks up, Tommy gets up from his seat and walks over to where Jim and Jacob are seated. As everyone starts to disperse around the bar, he motions both men in close. He solemnly looks at Jim and Jacob and pulls out a document from his jacket pocket. "I really had a hard time wrapping my head around what I'm going to tell you both. I put this together after Cozumel, mainly from the intel we gathered in the investigation we did when we vetted Jacob and your family for allowing him into my program, but it never really made sense to me until today."

Jacob leans into Tommy. "What are you talking about, Captain?"

Tommy sits down on a barstool and lets out a big breath of air. "I don't know any other way to say this, so I'll just tell you two the facts. We were able to piece together that during an altercation with the Sheridan County Sheriff's Department, the men you called Pack Leader and Grinder were killed. Al Freeburger was vague at best as to how they died or who was responsible. We just wrote it off as him having done it himself but not wanting any credit, which from his reputation would have been very believable. But then came Cozumel, and you fought and killed Dominik Thrace."

Jim interjects. "What does that have to do with those biker scum back in '74, Tommy?"

Tommy smiles, shakes his head, and laughs. "Actually, Jim, everything. You see, most criminals use aliases to operate in different areas. Your Pack Leader, otherwise known as Seth Brown, was a retired Marine Corps captain, who also had another alias that he used while conducting business in the Caribbean. In fact, during one of those business adventures, he met and married a young Jamaican woman. They had a son in 1972. The mother named that son Dominique, after her father, but the boy retained his father's last name, which in Jamaica at the time was Thrace." He pauses to let the implication of what he said settle in, then looks at both men. "So, two of the most notorious criminals of their generations were father and son. They were both beaten and killed independently by you two, another father and son. The coincidence here is mind-boggling, I know, but true."

Father and son look into one another's eyes and both grab and hug each other. Jim pulls back from his son and sees that only Joe and his immediate family could hear what Tommy had just said. He winks and says, "Let's all just keep this bit of information between us."

Everyone wholeheartedly agrees.

Tommy reaches in his pocket and pulls out Al's letter again and hands it to Jim. "You know, I've been wanting to hear this story ever since I got this from Al. I'm sorry that I didn't show it to you first. I just wanted to find out for myself."

Jim grabs the letter and reads it, shakes his head, laughs, and wipes a tear from his eye. He hands the letter to his son, looks over at Joe and laughs some more as he says, "Lieutenant Freeburger sure was a salty old bastard. Even Sheriff Manning couldn't win an argument with him to save his life, but he was like a second father to me."

Just then a voice booms, "Me too, especially when he would yell at me to try and be more like you, and then turn around and tell me to stop trying to be like you. It got confusing."

Everyone turns around to the back of the bar to see Sheriff Tim Becker and his wife, Beth, standing at the door. With them is his sister, Megan, and her husband, Sam. Jim and Linda are immediately on their feet to go over and hug Jim's cousins. Tim's face, though rugged and weather-burned, has no traces of the scars Grinder put on him, and Megan is sporting a full head of beautiful red hair.

After the biker attacks, Sheriff Manning suggested to the parents of the victims that the teenagers should get together and talk about what happened to them. He volunteered to supervise the session. Obviously, some romances and, later, marriages sprang from that suggestion. The three couples walk back together to the main part of the bar and begin mingling with others.

Joe Mason gets a phone call on his cell. His wife, Marcy, who used to work at the Wagon Box in Story, is calling to see why he is staying so late. When she hears that all the Edwards are in town and hanging out at the Rainbow Bar, she gets in her car and heads over.

A young, pretty girl in her mid-twenties walks up and introduces herself to Jim and Linda. "Mr. and Mrs. Edwards, my name is Megan Jones. I'm a reporter for the *Sheridan Tribune*. I heard

Joe Mason's story tonight, and I was wondering if you would give me permission to write and print it?"

Before Jim can respond, Jacob is on his feet and steps between the reporter and his dad. With a jovial but wicked smile, he laughs and says, "I think that's a fantastic idea. It's about time Dad has his story told, at least here in Sheridan."

Megan turns beet-red and is barely able to respond. "Uh, Commander Edwards, I would love to include any statements you'd like to offer, as well."

Jacob looks her straight in the eye but with a smile of his own. "Not on your life. I'm sick of being in the spotlight. It's Dad's turn."

Everyone, including Little Roberto, winds up staying way too late at the bar that night. Finally, Danielle and Chris remind them that they have an early flight out of the Sheridan airport in the morning. Danielle is especially anxious to get to South Texas, because Marnia Gonzalez asked her to be her maid of honor at her wedding. Jacob was taking the father of the bride's place and would be walking Marnia down the aisle. Jonathan asked Chris to be a groomsman, as Major Amilio Rohos, the head of the Mexican Anti-Cartel Task Force, was asked to be the best man.

One week later, the same day as the wedding, the *Sheridan Tribune* runs a front-page story titled "The Legend of Deputy Jim."

Much to Jim's dismay, a few other news sources around the country pick up on the story and run it as well.

The End

CPSIA information can be obtained
at www.ICGtesting.com
Printed in the USA
BVHW072309170919
558626BV00003B/17/P

9 780578 568324